Also in the *X Libris* series:

Back in Charge	Mariah Greene
The Discipline of Pearls	Susan Swann
Hotel Aphrodisia	Dorothy Starr
Arousing Anna	Nina Sheridan
Playing the Game	Selina Seymour
The Women's Club	Vanessa Davies
A Slave to His Kiss	Anastasia Dubois
Saturnalia	Zara Devereux
Shopping Around	Mariah Greene
Dares	Roxanne Morgan
Dark Secret	Marina Anderson
Inspiration	Stephanie Ash
Rejuvenating Julia	Nina Sheridan
The Ritual of Pearls	Susan Swann
Midnight Starr	Dorothy Starr
The Pleasure Principle	Emma Allan
Velvet Touch	Zara Devereux
Acting it Out	Vanessa Davies
The Gambler	Tallulah Sharpe
Musical Affairs	Stephanie Ash
Sleeping Partner	Mariah Greene
Eternal Kiss	Anastasia Dubois
Forbidden Desires	Marina Anderson
Pleasuring Pamela	Nina Sheridan
Letting Go	Cathy Hunter
Two Women	Emma Allan
Sisters Under the Skin	Vanessa Davies
Blue Notes	Stephanie Ash
Pleasure Bound	Susan Swann
Educating Eleanor	Nina Sheridan
Silken Bonds	Zara Devereux

Fast Learner

Ginnie Bond

An *X Libris* Book

First published by X Libris in 1997

Copyright © Ginnie Bond 1997

The moral right of the author has been asserted.

*All characters in this publication are
fictitious and any resemblance to real
persons, living or dead, is purely coincidental.*

All rights reserved.
No part of this publication may be reproduced,
stored in a retrieval system, or transmitted, in
any form or by any means, without the prior
permission in writing of the publisher, nor be
otherwise circulated in any form of binding or
cover other than that in which it is published and
without a similar condition including this condition
being imposed on the subsequent purchaser

A CIP catalogue record for this book
is available from the British Library.

ISBN 0 7515 1959 6

Photoset in North Wales by
Derek Doyle & Associates, Mold, Flintshire
Printed and bound in Great Britain by
Clays Ltd, St Ives plc

X Libris
A Division of
Little, Brown and Company (UK)
Brettenham House
Lancaster Place
London WC2E 7EN

Chapter One

FERNE DAVILLE WALKED up the grand staircase as sedately as she could, her breathing short, her pulses pounding in her temples.

Below her in the ballroom, revellers cavorted to a heavy rock beat. A kaleidoscope of flashing lights danced on naked skins and laughing faces lit with the ecstasy of champagne.

Bare-breasted young women in grassy skirts swayed erotically before their partners while others cavorted in body stockings poured around nubile forms. Clad in fantasy-dress, Superman, Batman, and the Six-Million-Dollar Man were there, their hired identities designed to cover a rash of blushes in the sober light of morning. My God – if only she had known that it was to be this kind of party she —

Sensing a man close behind her, Ferne slowed her pace despite her inner urge to run. She would not allow herself to be flustered by any man.

As the stairway curved towards the top, she glimpsed him, the blackness of his cape flowing from broad shoulders, its lining flickering in the light from chandeliers.

Ferne strode along the corridor with as much decorum as she could muster. But, as her losing race finished at her bedroom door, the pursuer took her by the waist, and playfully bit her neck.

'No.' She struggled. 'Please . . .'

Strong hands cupped her breasts now, fanned widely on her stomach, ran down her flanks, and slipped over her mons, all too prominent in the tightness of her Catwoman suit. He bit her neck once more and kissed her ear.

Her head went back reflexively. 'No. Please. You mustn't. I don't . . .'

Her plea was stifled as he spun her, his lips covering hers hotly, his mouth pliant yet insistent. She gasped and tried to push at him, his abdomen a firm expanse of well-trained muscles rippling as he breathed. The world began to whirl. And then the door gave way against their weight so that they fell in a tangle of arms and legs clad in tight, black Lycra.

Ferne squealed. 'No – please don't. You . . .'

He laughed widely as his lips descended once again. Now her mouth opened with her panting, anxiety and a strangely exciting expectation running through her. She fought him bravely, his hand clamped on her neck, the other working slowly at her breast. But she quietened at the warmth of champagne-sweet breath, and at the whispered sound of 'My god, you're beautiful.'

Sapphire eyes behind his mask closed for the

briefest moment. Ferne's eyes closed as well. For a moment, the world seemed to stop, with only the thump of heart pressed against heart, beating to the tempo of the music below.

Caressing fingers on her nipples, a knee between her legs, the hardness of the man's erection pushed urgently against her thigh, brought Ferne back to the reality of the scene. Into a black space in her mind sprang injunctions ingrained over painful years, reinforced with remembered beatings and cries of *dirty slut*.

Wriggling hard, Ferne pulled away. She crouched and spat, her green eyes flashing through the eye-holes of her mask. And as she ranged before the man, her fingers formed long claws and the black ears of her helmet pricked just like those of a feral cat.

She hissed, 'Don't you dare touch me again.'

He leaned back against the door, laughing with amusement. He stood with legs astride, the mask hiding all but the lower part of his face. But his outfit was so sheer and tight it left nothing of his muscular body to her imagination.

'Hello, pussycat.' He grinned and fixed her eyes with his, and placed long-fingered hands upon his hips. These led her attention towards the taut stomach, pumping from exertion. Then, as her gaze sank lower, she felt a flush crawl up her neck and burn her cheeks.

Barely disguised beneath his tights, the taut ridge of his erection curved up towards the panting navel. Within fractions of a second, Ferne's nerves were thrilling. She sensed the surfaces of her inner thighs taking up an impulse from her solar plexus. The tingle ran deep down, stirring little tremors in her womb which were not entirely unknown to her of late.

'What do you want?' The words sounded weak in the quietness of the bed chamber. She had known the answer before she even asked the question.

The wide mouth flashed a smile. 'I want whatever it is that you want, pussycat.'

Ferne's mind whirred as her body pulsed. Her mouth went very dry. What did she really want? Together, they had laughed and danced in the mêlée of the party. When he had pulled her tightly to himself, enveloping her in the black and scarlet of his Batman cloak, she had felt the heat and firmness of his body. At first she had gasped and tried to pull away, but he'd held her fast, looking down into her eyes before lowering that sensual mouth to hers. And then she'd felt his hardness against her pubis. The rush of sensual heat up her neck, over her cheeks and out to the tips of her ears had been like a bush fire, burning away the prickly protection she had grown around herself. She had thanked God that — under her cat mask and hood — no one in the crowd knew who she was.

'I thought you wanted me to follow you.' His voice was resonant and kind, with just a thread of humour running through a Scottish brogue.

Ferne felt vulnerable yet exhilarated. Her heart still pounded from her flight. But far from escaping from the man, she was trapped in an isolated bedroom of the castle, at a party she had been hijacked into, and in a too-revealing suit she had been almost forced to wear. Unable to cover up her breasts or hide her prominent mons, she felt quite naked. The suit conspired to bring every inch of her skin to a level of unaccustomed sensitivity. This was heightened by his admiring looks, and his all-too-obvious readiness to strip her and to take her there and then.

He smiled again, braced strong, athletic legs apart and kept the blue eyes on her own. 'So what do you want?'

'I want to go to bed.'

His mouth curved slightly at her gaffe but he didn't say a word.

'I meant that I came up to get away from the party.' The tremor in Ferne's voice undermined the authority of her words. There was a slight shrug of the broad shoulders as the blue eyes took on a knowing sparkle. He was enjoying her discomfiture. Damn him – he had her mesmerised.

For once Ferne felt disconcerted. Usually she was so cool with men. It was a matter of good schooling, of being brought up to be careful about what she said to them, about how she behaved and – most of all – of being wary of their ambitions.

You'll have them coming out of the woodwork, girl, her father had gasped on his deathbed. *And you'll never know if it's you or the Daville fortune they're really after. Stay single. Keep control.*

She had stayed single, but years of keeping

control had set her apart from her contemporaries. She was not like her women friends, their eyes brilliant with the light of excitement as they flitted through life. Like exotic moths they were sedentary by day, alive and fluttering at night-time, brightly coloured in their designer originals, sparkling with diamonds and gold, cocooned in the ivory leather of exorbitantly expensive cars. All was show. All was calculated to dazzle the eye and to mesmerise the mind of some wealthy young buck. Love did not come into their equations. Fun, sex, and drink were the fuel they seemed to need and they attracted it by the bucketful. Most were not happy with it. Several had destroyed themselves in its acquisition.

'You're very tempting. But I think you know that.'

The man's words snapped Ferne back to the hard reality of his presence. She tossed her head back haughtily. 'You don't know what I look like.' Now she pulled her mask and cat-eared cap protectively around her face. She had purposely kept it on all night. That way, no one would know that Ferne Daville had deigned to join the riotous, drunken orgy which Fanni Deighton-Smythe had thrown for her affected friends.

But you'll love it, darling, Fanni had boomed. *It's about time you started to live. You can't bury yourself in ledgers and share certificates all your life. And by the look of you, you need a bit of the hard stuff.*

Ferne had shot her a puzzled glance, saying, *You know I don't drink.*

Fanni had thrown her head back in theatrical laughter. *My god, Ferne Daville; I didn't mean booze. Haven't you had it yet?*

No, she hadn't had 'It'. She had heard about it from friends. But the stories which they told were no better than fisherman's tales. The more often they were spun, the bigger and harder and longer and the more curved and veiny the 'It' seemed to become.

But now, with legs apart and hands on hips, Ferne defied the Scotsman presenting her with 'It' for the first time in her life. And as she stared at it, her body was rebelling with the sensations the sight created.

The man grinned; flashing a set of perfectly formed teeth. Behind the mask, the eyes shone brightly, as if reflecting the light of the smile. 'Isn't this what you came up for?' He stroked his penis provocatively, making it spring inside his tights.

She shook her head. 'I told you. I came up to get away from the noise.'

'You don't like parties?'

'I detest them.'

'Then why did you come?'

Ferne didn't know. But at twenty-five years old, she had found that she was fast gaining a reputation as an old maid. Men she knew no longer pestered her. She had erected prickly defences against any advances, even though the sight of attractive men seemed to set her alight so easily – especially pictures of attractively naked men. But she assumed that her would-be lovers all knew of her wealth and that they were only after a share of it, just as her women friends hunted rich and eligible males. But, despite all the battening-down of sensations she had done of late, she was finding it increasingly difficult to maintain her indifference to the stimulation they evoked deep inside her.

Her eyes snapped back on to his face and tried to hold there, but they could not help making an occasional foray downwards. Two large ovals beneath the strong, thick ridge seemed to have drawn up tight beneath the shaft as it swelled to greater size. This tensed as he stood with legs widespread, and when he swung his hips towards her, it was as if he was doing it to hypnotise her with his essential maleness.

Ferne suddenly came to her normal, unflappable senses and recalled why she was in the bedroom. It must have been the intoxication of the adrenalin running through her that had sharpened her lust and dulled her reason for those few seconds. That and the champagne. She'd be safer in the crowd downstairs.

'Please let me pass.'

He raised a hand. 'You didn't answer my question. Why did you come here tonight if you don't like parties?'

'Fanni tricked me. When she invited me for the weekend, she didn't tell me she was having a fantasy-dress party.'

'But you seemed to be enjoying yourself so much. When we danced, I could have sworn that you were having a really good time. By the way you rubbed yourself against me, I thought you wanted something more than kisses.'

She had. But that must have been the influence of the champagne. She normally never drank it, but some fool had spiked her bitter lemon. At first she'd thought that it was just a different kind of bitter lemon; sweeter and more fizzy. Then her senses had come alive as a warm glow had spread throughout her body, heating up her skin, bringing tingles to her nipples, and a wonderfully curious tightness to her vulva. She had grabbed another sparkling glass from a passing silver tray and from then onwards the party had taken place in a very pleasant haze.

But now her head was clear again. Once more she snapped her eyes away from the ridge of the man's erection.

He shrugged at her, smiled once more and swung his hips towards her. 'And I suppose you don't like making love either.'

Trying hard not to be daunted by the proximity of the taut male body, Ferne jerked herself up as tall as she could manage, pulling in a deep breath too. 'I know what you're after. All you're interested in is my . . .'

'Your body?' As the blue eyes watched her closely through the eye-slits in his mask, he put her at a disadvantage.

Now her confidence ebbed away with each wave of sensation rushing upwards from the vee of her parted legs, rippling over the tenseness of her stomach and driving her nipples to hardness.

In the tightness of her catsuit she could feel her secret lips pulsing with the rhythm of her heartbeat. Of late they had done that when she had been aroused, swelling so that the sexual mouth they protected felt a fullness she had never sensed before. Now she was aware that the detail of those lips showed through the sheer material of her tights. It made her feel so wanton. The strange, insistent need drove her into situations she would never have contemplated under normal circumstances. But those 'normal circumstances' were asexual. Surrounded by fawning and somewhat elderly men, she had never given the slightest thought to their sexuality. She was the boss in the company and that was all there was to be said about it. They did as they were told. Now, in the heat of this bedroom, the circumstances were quite different. Something in her told her that this man would not take the kind of orders she was accustomed to giving out.

She was trapped.

He blocked her way and barred the door, and by the way he defied her, she understood that he was not about to be moved easily. Then, to her uneasy excitement, he moved towards her in the moonlight.

'Yes I want your body. But if it's not a come-on, why are you wearing that revealing suit?'

Ferne crossed her arms tightly. 'I didn't mean my body. I meant my money.' It was snapped out, just as she would snap her disagreements down the length of the boardroom table, watching the recoil from ranks of grey-faced men.

In the gloaming, Ferne saw the eyes slit behind the Batman mask. The head went sharply back. It was as if he were trying to make sense of her outburst.

She placed her slender hands upon her hips, mimicking his posture of defiance. Or was it sheer bravado? She didn't feel defiant or brave; just annoyed. But despite her tone, she was melting. Despite her annoyance, her heart pumped from the sensations the sexual readiness of his body was instilling in her.

He scratched his skullcap. 'I'm sorry. I don't follow. What money are you talking about? I'm not a burglar and I'm not after that kind of treasure.'

His voice had a mellow, cultured tone which would turn a woman's head in any gathering. The Scottish lilt seemed to resonate from somewhere deep behind the muscular stomach. It reminded her of a voice she knew, but she could not quite place him, or bring a face to mind.

'Don't pretend that you don't know who I am.' She shook her head to reinforce the assertion.

He put back his head and laughed aloud. 'I don't care a damn who you are, pussycat. I don't care if you're the Queen of Sheba or Cleopatra. All I know is that your body's telling me quite clearly that you want me to strip you and take you to bed.'

'Then your imagination's running away with you.'

'Is it?'

Suddenly the eyes lost their mischief and turned

to hurt, though Ferne was not at all convinced that it was genuine. Perhaps the look was created to soften her resistance. But she did soften. Then she hardened again. This situation was getting out of hand. She had allowed her desire to run away with her common sense.

'I don't do that.'

'What don't you do?'

'I don't "go to bed" with your sort.' It was blurted. Defensive. Insensitive. She knew so very little about him, so how could she categorise him as any 'sort'? Then she corrected her last thought. She did know that he was a very stimulating sort of man. He was a Scottish Highlands stag, proud in the way he held his head up and in the way he thrust his pelvis out, presenting himself to her; certain of his masculinity, definite in every movement.

Suddenly she was scared. She was scared of her reaction to him and her loss of control of the situation. 'Please let me pass.'

He caught her arms as she tried to push him aside. 'Oh no, you cold little pussycat. I don't know who you are but you don't give me the come-on and then slam the door on me.'

His mouth was on her neck before she could push him away. He bit her tenderly and breathed her black hair as it spilled out from under her cat-eared hood. Ferne quivered, contact with him again setting waves of energy coursing through her womb. The inner surfaces of her thighs seemed to burn. And she was liquid with a sensitising moisture she could not control either.

'Please.' Her voice trembled as her body shook.

'Please what, pussycat?' He dipped his head to her cheek and kissed her softly, whispering, 'Please make love to me?' Then, as the mouth came down to hers, Ferne went quite limp in the enclosing arms. At first the kiss was fleeting, as if he were testing her. And when she did not fight back, he came again, the lips working hers in delightful, rhythmic movements. Then, as her lips came alive for only the second time in her life, her breath began to pant.

Now he increased his pressure, one arm tightening around her shoulders, the other around her waist. The pressure of his erection against her pubis increased as his hand slipped over her bottom, the fingers working in concert with his lips.

Against her best injunctions her legs opened. She wanted to feel him there. Her secret lips wanted contact with his shaft. They wanted to sense it and to rub along its length.

Now his fingers ran up and down her spine, fanning out then diving between the cheeks of her buttocks so intimately that she gasped.

She was trapped by his powerful grip, by his insistent mouth, and by the scent and allure of him. He was an enigma behind that mask. And behind her own mask she felt safe. She might let herself go and no one would know that Ferne Daville – the iceberg – had at last melted under the sexual heat of a man. Something in her had wanted this from the moment he had whisked her into the swirling dance. He had said nothing at first.

Then, whispering words in her ear as he'd tightened his hold on her, he had set her pulses racing.

How do you like to make love? He had asked it with his lips against her cheek. *Long and soft and gently? Or – do you just want fucking hard, little pussycat?*

She had squirmed at the sensations the whisperings had conjured between her legs, but he had held her tightly. And every little squirm she had made had only served to work her more against the hardness beneath his tights.

I don't make love. She had turned her face away from him.

Never?

Never!

I don't believe you. The way you move shouts to me that your body craves it. Do you deny what it says?

Yes, she had always denied what her body said.

As they had smooched, he had whispered, *Do you like to be kissed all over?*

Again she had wriggled but it had been for the sake of propriety, not to get away now.

Shall I make love to you right here on the dance floor? Shall I strip away this slinky suit and suck your nipples, and bite your pretty neck. Shall I lay you down and spread your legs to lick you slowly up the insides of your thighs?

At that she had trembled. That would have been so humiliating even though there had been couples already rhythmically engrossed in various parts of the ballroom and on the moonlit terrace outside.

Or shall I carry you off to bed?

At that, she had fled.

Now his lips worked hers more avidly. His tongue made a little foray as she opened her mouth to breathe. The tip of her own tongue touched his, withdrew and touched again. Now they fenced. Her legs felt just like jelly. Her stomach heaved. Her heart pounded and her pelvis thrust outwards as they kissed. There seemed to be a line of energy which ran from her lips to her breasts. From the erect nipples, that line of fire flashed downwards, connecting electrically with the nub of her clitoris she had fondly touched of late. This swelled and throbbed as if it were coming alive like her lips, becoming so sensitive as it burgeoned from its sheath. It wanted to be touched more openly. It wanted to be kissed. She had read that women could have wonderful feelings when a man put his mouth to that part of her and kissed and sucked and teased at it. It was an experience which she had never allowed herself to have. Even now, he might be seducing her for her wealth. As she progressively gave up control of herself, she might be sliding on the nursery slopes of naïvety, into an avalanche of experiences she would regret.

But what the hell? It was time to grow up. It was time she let her body have its way and experienced those things her imagination had been conjuring for months. Fanni had remonstrated with her for years about her sexual reticence. Now at last she was doing it. But she was doing it incognito. Afterwards, she could get up and walk away, and he would never know who he had made love to.

He would not be any threat to her fortune because he would never know that he had bedded the seventh richest woman in the country.

Ferne did not feel her full-length zip slide. It was the coolness on her back which warned her that he'd slipped it. Now the warmth of his hand on her bottom contrasted with that coolness. It slipped up and down her back, the fingers spreading and closing as it went.

His lips still held hers. But hers were harrying his every time he tried to pull away. With her mouth placed sideways for fuller access, she was devouring him, her tongue lashing at his, her fingers clawing at his back. Then her mouth went on a foray of small biting movements over his face and neck before returning to take his mouth again.

A few minutes more found her naked to the waist, the black Lycra of Fanni's catsuit hanging loosely. Her hips undulated against his, set in motion by the need to feel him, her legs wide so that she could press against the ridge of hardness she needed to capture. She needed to rub it against her clitoris. All her attention was focussed by its need.

His calf-length boots were shed, the cloak cast to the ground, and as he stood back and fixed her eyes, he slid out of his suit, sloughing it as smoothly as a snake removes its skin. And now he stood proudly, naked of all but the Batman mask and hood. The shaft of flesh between his legs reared like a cobra. Curving up towards his navel, it erupted from a matt of golden hair. At the sight of the man's phallus so close to her, Ferne's stomach fluttered uncontrollably, like aspen leaves in a summer breeze. The glossy, flat organs she had looked at secretly in Fanni's magazines seemed innocuous by comparison with this. None of the colour plates or the descriptions from friends had prepared her for the fleshy reality of a man's full-blown erection, the smooth and plummy helmet perched upon such a rigid shaft.

Soft and curiously wrinkled, its pouch moved with his breathing, its softness contrasting strongly with the firmness of the shaft. This seemed already to have grown another inch since she had fixed her gaze upon it. How big could it get?

He moved in close, slipping his hands about her shoulders, pulling her so that she fell towards him without any protest. Now her breasts rode his chest, hard against her nipples. The sweat of their rising passion lubricated their skins, sensitising the erect buds so that even the pink-brown nimbuses stood proud.

The sensation of his hot skin against hers set up a tension throughout her body, her breasts becoming pleasantly tight with the stimulation. Her waist felt taut, as did her stomach. And the tension of her tights pulled at her secret lips until she felt them opening, slippery and highly sensitised to every little touch. She wanted to feel him there. Her primal instinct wanted this man deep inside her.

Her leg came up around his hip, so that she could force his thigh between her own legs, widening the lips of her sex to feel his heat through her Lycra.

'So – do you want me to fuck you hard or to love you gently?' It was so simply said, as if he were asking white or red wine at dinner? Then he let out a hiss of a smile. He was teasing her. She bit his neck hard, unable to say her needs in words.

'All right,' he whispered, 'shall I have you by the door, or shall we use the bed?' Now he raked deeply under her raised thigh and growled. As the fingertips ran across her labia, she shuddered. But still she didn't answer, her hands clawing at his back, the muscles under her fingers rippling as he bent to run a line of love-bites down her neck. And when both strong hands slipped inside her tights, pushing them slowly downwards, she trembled with the anticipation of her most private self becoming naked to him. But as she stepped out of the wrinkled pile about her ankles, Ferne felt proud and threw her head back, her breasts thrust outwards.

Now his lips were against her pubis. My God, he was kissing her there. Her hands wrapped around his head, his skullcap covering curly hair beneath. What colour hair? Blond? Yes; like his golden pubis. What Scotsman did she know with gold and curly hair?

His hands worked up her bottom, pulling her on to his mouth. She widened her legs reflexively, bending her knees, thrusting her pelvis forward, throwing her head back, her eyes closed, her mouth panting open.

Hell, she wanted him even more.

An electric shock ran through her as she felt his

tongue. It explored her tentatively just as it had explored her mouth. Now she trembled from head to toe. She opened her legs wider, her hands kneading at his head as her pelvis thrust further forward, her breasts so tight that she felt every little movement as she swung them to and fro.

As the tongue came again, she rocked herself, working up and down on it by springing her knees.

Now she felt the tickling sensation as he took an excursion to the hollows beside her engorged sex-lips before returning to her clitoris. This was throbbing more now in tiny little heartbeats of fullness – of lustfulness. It was erect, almost painfully sensitive. But it still needed harsher treatment. She wanted to feel him stronger, not to be lapped. This was wonderful but there was a pressure building deep inside her which her instinct told her would only be released by greater and more forceful contact.

His fingers raked her thighs, each stroke of his nails setting a trail of fire in her skin.

'Oh my God,' she whispered as tears came to her eyes, and her whole body began to quiver. Then he rose and placed a line of little licks up her stomach to her breasts. Each nipple was taken in its turn, teased tenderly with in-turned lips as they pulled and sucked her into ecstasy.

Now he came upwards again, lip-biting her under her chin until he found her mouth panting with the sensation of what he had done to her body.

'Fuck me.' She was almost shocked at herself as the words escaped from her mind and hissed through her parted lips before her sense of propriety could rein them in.

Without a word, he moved away, cradled her strongly and laid her on the bed. On top of her, he held his weight on his arms, only his body from the hips downwards touching hers.

She opened her legs to him now, desperately needing to feel him inside her. But he slipped his hardness gently over her labia. She arched her back, straining her body up to his, trying to make him enter her. Her instinct drove her need, seeming to know without tuition that she must swallow his hard length to get the sensation she needed. But he only slid it over her sex-lips, each stroke ploughing lushly through her groove, each heave of her pelvis pressing her clitoris hard against the shaft.

He was goading her. Torturing her.

'Mmmmmmm.' Slick with sweat, her body heaved against him, her sex-mouth trying to capture him at every tantalising stroke, her legs scissoring in the effort. Then she wound her legs around his tensed thighs. Thus she opened her sex wide so that she could sense him better, just as she had wanted to do from the minute she had felt him on the dance floor. Now he lowered his athletic body on to hers as if he were doing press-ups. Centimetre by centimetre she felt his heat as he let it settle along the whole of her length. He took her arms above her head, long fingers weaving between her own as he pressed her hands deep into the covers. With his elbows against hers he pinned her to the bed, his mouth working at her lips again, her breasts sliding against his chest.

As their nipples kissed and pressed together, she yearned for more and she fought even harder to capture him. She fought for air, and she fought to give herself up to him, sighing, 'Oh my God. Oh my God. Please fuck me.'

That word was a word she had abhorred. It was a crude, hole-in-the-corner word for sluts and sniggering jokes. But now it was the only word to use. She could not ask for love. He was not loving her; he was a total stranger. He was having her. She was having him. She wanted to have him, to feel him, to feel and to know what sex was. She wanted that shaft inside her. She needed it and she would go mad if she did not feel it soon. Her body was contorted in paroxysms of desire, her nerve endings alive with a strange electricity which made her gasp with every stroke of his skin against her own. She could feel the hair of his heavy pouch as he came to the end of his upward stroke. His testicles brushed her anus. Even this was yearning to be touched.

She strained again, her legs around his waist, her ankles interlocked. 'Please?'

'Please what, pussycat?'

'You know.'

'Say it again.' His shaft bore down on her, pushing her clitoris upwards, stretching it, making it ache with pleasure-pain. And as his scrotum nudged at the drum-tight membranes of her loins, Ferne began to shudder uncontrollably.

She raked his back with her nails and threw her head from side to side, tears running hotly down her cheeks. 'Fuck me,' she croaked. 'I can't stand this any longer.'

Chapter Two

FERNE STIFLED a scream as a sharp pain shot through her body, blasting away that last barrier she had maintained against becoming a complete woman.

Music in the rooms below thumped throughout the castle. Lights cascaded in her head. The base beat matched the thumping of her heart which matched in turn the thump of the man's pubis against her own. Her clitoris was crushed with every stroke, receiving the punishing it seemed to need, the tension in it building to an explosive pitch.

He didn't show her violence, but he pinned her to the bed and drove into her so powerfully that she juddered with the force of it.

Her pelvic muscles began to tense and close upon the shaft she had wanted to caress and put her lips to. Now as he drove into her, she opened up her legs and stretched them wide. Then, as he drew out again, she clamped him hard. This seemed to make him work more urgently. He was losing his self-control, just as she had lost her own.

'Harder,' she whispered in his ear as his teeth bit at her shoulder. She shuddered at the bolt of pleasure-pain it sent rushing through her, inciting him to raise his tempo.

From the ballroom far below them came a deeper, faster beat. It was as if their hostess were playing an accompaniment to their sex. They were not making love. It was plain, old-fashioned sexual intercourse and it was more marvellous than any experience Ferne had had in all her life. She knew she'd been a fool to deny her needs for so long.

Now, as his thrusts became more urgent, he lifted her from the springing bed so that her sex was presented upwards, and he could drive down into her even harder.

'Fuck me,' she whispered. It made her thrill, and saying that word seemed to goad him more. So she whispered it repeatedly, wanting greater pace, more force, more pressure, and more of the wonderful pain it brought her inner core. That pain was building now, but was being held in check, unable to rage through her and escape.

'Oh my God. Please fuck me.' Now she screamed it; uncaring if anyone heard her. 'Oh, that's so beautiful.'

He took her with a rising passion which made her breasts quiver. She clawed his back and raked his thighs. Violently she closed upon the straining shaft. But as he withdrew it from her and stopped, she cried out, 'What the hell are you stopping for?'

'I haven't got a condom.'

'Damn the condom – I'm on the pill.'

Without a second's pause he took her, pumping into her with such power that she gasped. And then she felt his fluid heat deep inside her. It set a fire which flickered in her core.

For the first time in her life, Ferne felt a man's ejaculation. The walls of her vagina began to ripple, each small wave so wonderful that she tossed her head and moaned. And then came the avalanche of intense sensations as her whole body went into rigor. Her back arched, and her sex closed on the shaft. Then her back relaxed and her head went back as she sucked air with the pleasurable pain of it all, gasping, 'Oh my God. My God.' And then the rigor came again.

Panting together, they lay enmeshed, smaller ripples of energy running through Ferne to him and back again. And still he beat inside her.

Her hand stroked the muscles of his back, her fingers finding a prominent mole at the bottom of his spine.

He pushed inside her vulva, and he kissed her slender neck.

She pecked his cheek and closed her eyes, basking in the heat of his body and the tickling of his balls as they nestled against the folds of her sex-lips. He had taken her so uncompromisingly. He had read her inner feelings and reacted to them, refusing to be rebuffed by her put-offs. And still he did not know who she was. Thank God.

She didn't know him either, even though something under his Scottish accent struck a note of recognition but refused to come forward as a picture in her mind. Both of them had kept their masks on. Both had kept the secret of their identity. They might do this again. And if they did, with the anonymity of the masks, the Daville fortune would be safe. There would be no risk that he wanted her wealth instead of her. Anyway, they might be well suited. Perhaps they could meet clandestinely and screw at first and then gradually learn more and more about each other. They might even fall in love. Then, and only then, might she take off the mask.

As she lay impaled by the man, Ferne thought of that magic word again. Fuck. She sounded it in her head. Under the pressure of the building orgasm, she had said it over and over. Each time it had increased his passion. Each time she had felt more abandoned, more wanton, more a sexual creature than the cold and calculating guardian of the Daville estates and assets. The word had lost its crudity. It was as if it had been an empty shell of a word which had become filled with all those delightful feelings which had welled within her.

'Fuck.' She whispered it to herself, hardly aloud. It was just like magic. Already she wanted to do it again.

He rested on his elbows, looking down into her eyes, studying her intently with a query. 'What did you say?'

She smiled. 'I was just thinking aloud, that's all.' For a moment she had the impulse to reach up and remove his mask. But that would have spoiled the fun. It would have broken the spell. And it might have ruined any future adventures they might have. She didn't know if Ferne Daville could behave like this. It had been the Catwoman who had lost her cool and had abandoned herself to sex, not Ferne Louise Marie-Anne Daville.

'Are you OK?' He brushed her face with his finger-tips.

She kissed them very lightly. 'I'm wonderfully OK. And thanks for not taking any notice of my outburst. I would have been devastated if you'd turned and gone.'

He kissed her lips. 'I'm glad I let Johnny Stiff have his head then. He sat up and took notice as soon as you walked into the room in that cat outfit.'

'You, sir, are a philanderer.'

He tapped her nose. 'I, miss, am a very discerning man. I don't go bedding every woman who crosses my path.'

'But you do bed some, I'm sure.'

He smiled and flashed those sparkling teeth again. And then he kissed her long and tenderly, his hand wandering over her hair. 'And what about you? Do you often mesmerise men with those Cleopatra eyes and lure them to your boudoir?'

'I never lure men to my boudoir. You're the f—' She closed her eyes. She hadn't meant to tell him that.

'You're not telling me I'm your first?'

She nodded.

'You're a virgin?'

Now she smiled demurely. 'Was a virgin, I think is the appropriate tense.'

He closed his eyes. 'Bloody hell. If I'd realised, I would have . . .'

She stroked his face, her hands itching to get under the mask again. 'You would have what? Run away?'

He shook his head and fondled one of her breasts, the thumb and forefinger working at the nipple. It made her begin to thrill again.

'No, I wouldn't have run away. But I would have been more gentle with you.'

'You were perfect.'

'Thank you, ma'am. I'm glad it was good for your first time.'

She reached up and kissed him tenderly. 'I wouldn't have wanted it any other way. I dreaded ever getting married. The thought of doing it from cold on my wedding night petrified me.'

'You're engaged?'

She grinned. 'Right now I am, but not in the way you mean.' She squeezed him hard between her legs and then she kissed his nose.

He withdrew his penis gently from her, slipped down her body, and took a nipple between his lips. As his tongue circled round the nimbus, Ferne felt a pleasant tingling in her clitoris.

'If you do that much more, you'll start me off again.'

'Do you want to be started off again?'

She smiled and turned her head away. Then she turned back. Why did she need to be so coy? He did not know who she was. Besides, he was being the most intimate he could be with her after only an hour's acquaintance. His mouth was on her stomach now, kissing at her skin. His hand slipped deep between her open legs.

The slight touch of a finger upon her throbbing bud was marvellous. She opened her legs wider. She wanted to abandon herself to him again. She wanted him to look at her, intimately, to see how succulent her lips were, and how they folded inwards.

He ran his tongue deeply through her cleft.

'Mmmmm.' She put her head back and gave a little shudder of delight. He looked up over her black-haired mons, between her full breasts, whispering, 'Hell, you're beautiful.' Then he ran his hand over her stomach, outlined her waist and skimmed her hip-bones.

'You're just saying that to get round me.' She gave a little laugh.

He ran his finger up the inside of her leg, caressed the hollow between her loin and her secret lips and worked her clitoris gently once again.

'Mmmmmm. I like that.'

'There you are,' he whispered, increasing his finger's movement over her thrilling bud. 'I don't need to say anything to get round you.'

'You're a devil.'

He shook his head, the mouth smiling gently. 'I know a bit about women, that's all.'

'Chauvinist pig.'

Pulling himself up the bed, he lay beside her. Then he took her mouth, working so continuously that Ferne had to breathe through her nostrils. His hand took her firmly between the legs, the heel of his thumb hard against her pubis, the middle finger curling deep inside her. Two outer fingers worked the hollows each side of the lips as the whole hand moved slowly up and down.

Immediately Ferne felt her hips rising. She bent her knees to a right angle, the sole of each foot flat against the other. She needed to feel him gripping her intimately. It was such a totally forbidden thing to do and she was revelling in it. She was rebelling against all the old taboos.

'Ahhhh,' she inhaled deeply. 'That's too nice. Pig.'

'Then I'll stop – Strumpet.' He laughed a carefree laugh.

'Don't you dare stop. When I abandon myself to lust for the first time in my life, I'm not going to be short-changed. I want my money's worth.'

He stopped immediately. And she could smell her own muskiness on his fingers as he removed his hand from its delightful goading and took her chin angrily.

'There's no charge for this.'

Ferne could see the anger in his eyes. For the second time since finding him, she was frightened. She tried to smile, but it was wooden. 'I'm sorry. I didn't mean to . . .' She swallowed hard. 'Please don't stop now. It's just that this really is such a new experience for me. I don't know the first thing about having sex.'

'Or making love?' He kissed the tip of her nose, his anger seeming to have dissipated. 'But I'm dumbfounded. Where have you been since puberty? In a convent?'

She shook her head. It had been a self-imposed condition. No, that was not entirely true. She had been imprisoned by her father's dying words; scared that men would not want her for herself. But she had been wrong. This man had wanted her without knowing anything about her wealth.

He kissed her nose again. 'Do you really want to learn about sex?'

She nodded, tears coming to her eyes. 'I want to learn how to feel and how to give pleasure. I don't want to go on being prickly. Fanni says that I have a barbed-wire look that rips men's egos to shreds. I do want people to want me, even if it's only for wild sex. I don't want them to want me for my . . .' She stopped before she blurted out the word.

'For your what?'

'For anything else.' She turned her face aside.

'Why else would they want you?' He took her chin and made her face him. She tried to shake her head but he held her firmly. 'Do you want to experience all the sensations a woman can have? Do you want to learn how to love and be loved? Do you want the most lascivious kind of sex any woman could experience?'

'Do you want to teach me?'

'Answer my question.' He was masterly when he wanted something.

Ferne thought hard. This one experience seemed to have liberated her so much. As she lay there, she felt so different. She felt sensuous. She felt alive. Perhaps she should have done this earlier in her life instead of bottling up all the feelings she had had. Maybe that was what had made her so bad-tempered.

'I would like more of the same it that's what you mean.'

He smiled. 'Is that all?'

Now she frowned at him. Was he making fun of her? 'Isn't this all there is?'

He stroked her chin slowly with his forefinger. 'No, there can be a lot more to sex and love than this.' He ran his finger around her nipple and down into her navel, making her shudder with the pleasure that it brought her. 'I could introduce you to a whole new world, but it might be dangerous for you.'

'How dangerous?' she sighed.

'You might turn into a libertine. Once you loose the wanton woman in you, you might not be able to cage her again. Are you willing to take the risk?'

'I think I have to. I think I've kept her caged for too long.'

He moved Ferne so that she lay on top of him, her arms crossed; her elbows on his shoulders. Like this she could look directly into his eyes. The warmth of his breath flirted with her mouth, and as she bent to kiss him, her eyes closed, her breasts pressing his again.

'Do you know,' she whispered. 'I'm telling you

all my darkest secrets and I don't even know your name. What shall I call you?' It seemed incongruous that they had been so intimate and not even been introduced. Perhaps that was what had made it so exhilarating.

'You can call me whatever you like. I'll keep the name just for you.' He ran his fingers lightly down her spine and made her sex-lips tremor in a tiny spasm.

'Shall I call you Ernest?' You look very earnest at times,' she smiled.

He nudged her playfully, raking her back right down to her bottom. Her vaginal muscles clenched hard.

'How about Johnny?' she asked, touching her lips lightly to his, sensing the centre of her sex moving against his own. His cock stirred strongly against her labia. 'How about Johnny Stiff?'

'If he's going to be doing most of the work I suppose that would be appropriate,' he grinned and raked her back again. 'And I'll call you Cleopatra.'

'If you must.'

'It suits you, you green-eyed she-cat.'

'If you say so.'

'I do.' He bit her on the shoulder.

'And what do you do for a living, Johnny Stiff?'

'I'm a gigolo.' His mouth curved in a wide smile as he scratched her flank slowly, sending trickles of energy through her body.

She was not sure whether or not to believe that he was a gigolo. The smile and its reflected twinkle in his eyes showed that he was full of fun, so she went along with the game. 'And what does a gigolo do for his living?'

He reached up and kissed her tenderly. 'He makes love to beautiful women in ways that you might never believe possible.'

'Good. I'd like that. Are you expensive?' she giggled.

'Very expensive.'

'How much is "very"?' The businesswoman in her was suddenly alert.

He kissed her on the tip of the nose. 'That depends on what you want, Cleopatra.'

'I want everything. I want to know what I've been missing for so long.'

His eyes studied her steadily now, seeming to be puzzled at her manner. 'You're serious, aren't you?'

'I never fool around when I want something badly.'

Still he studied her, as if he was trying to make a decision. 'It would be very expensive to do it well. Could you afford it?'

Ferne was relieved. This was the confirmation that he didn't know who she was or that she was very rich. She could consort with him with total abandon and lose herself to his sexuality without the fear of wondering if he was after her money, or the Daville empire. Or if he was going to blackmail her. Or abduct her for a ransom.

'I can probably raise some cash. How much do you want?' Now it was serious. She was the negotiator. But this time she was bargaining for herself, not for some piece of real estate or the assets of a company to strip and sell.

'I'll let you know when I've thought about it.'

'When will that be?'

'All in good time.'

'But where shall we meet? When can we start? What will we do?'

He placed his finger across her lips. 'Shhh. I said, all in good time, Cleopatra. Then he slipped his shaft into her so easily and so deeply she was surprised. She was slick, and as he slid she felt the mushroom head ripple inside her. Then he took her into his arms, her mouth kissing at his neck, his hand smoothing at the hollow of her back. And as he swelled inside her, Ferne's body came to vibrant life again. She straddled his hard body so she could ride him, her fingers splayed on his chest, her arms ramrod stiff, her sex plunging over him as she raised and lowered her hips.

His hands sought out her breasts and cupped them in their palms, his thumbs and fingers pulling at the nipples.

That was beautiful. It shot bolts of tingling energy to her clitoris. She pushed down on him harder.

Synchronising his movements with hers as she raised herself, he withdrew. Then as she plunged down on him he drove up into her hard.

'Oh. My God. Ahhhh.' The inner surfaces of her thighs and her labia were so slick she had to clamp hard to feel the thick stem of veined flesh as it sought to discharge deep within her.

The creak of bed springs, the music down below,

his thrusting and the tempo of her riding built to a crescendo until she climaxed. Ferne felt herself flood, sensuously and hot. It was so intimately satisfying. She felt him tense then thrust upwards. Again she felt his steady beat, and his flush adding to her warmth.

'Ahhh.' She took a gulp of air, thrusting her breasts into his palms, her stomach muscles pulling sharply inwards, her head thrown back as she closed her eyes and clamped him.

They gave out their moans of pleasure together.

Sitting back upon him, she pulled him tight inside her, the hard shaft at a right angle to his body. And as she ran her hands across the tightness of her belly, she felt the gently ticking bulge which was his cockhead deep inside her. When she massaged it from the outside, he groaned and closed his eyes and pushed up hard.

'Witch.'

'Stud.' She rubbed again.

'You're learning fast, pussycat. I can see you'll be a good student.'

'And you a good tutor.' She sank on to his chest now, still coupled to his beating penis. It was so marvellous. It was so utterly permissive and caring. She had always feared men dominating her. That was one thing she could not have stood. To allow herself to become submissive by choice was one thing; to be taken by force and to be subjugated was quite another. Was that not why she had taken to the contraceptive pill since quite an early age? It gave her an insurance against unexpected attack. An heiress always carried the fear of abduction; the possibility of rape.

Also, the contraception gave her a certain amount of control over her monthly cycle so that she could always be at her best for the most important meetings. She would not be dominated in any way by men or by her own sexuality.

But this man had been neither totally dominating nor submissive. He had allowed her to experience him but had participated in her pleasure at the end. And when he had taken her, she had given herself, she had allowed him to do what she had needed so badly.

She slipped off him and into his arms. 'Is it always like this the first time?'

'Like what, pussycat?'

'Is it always so explosive at first and then dies away?'

He stroked the back of her catsuit hood. 'You *ain't* felt nothin' yet, babe.'

She laughed at his American drawl. 'My God – if it gets more violent than that I don't know if I'll survive it.'

As he let out a small laugh, she felt the air leave his mouth, sidle around her own and float into the warmness of the room. They lay sensing each other, the rumpus in the castle slowly quietening. The growl of powerful cars, and the rattle of the drawbridge, and the swish of tyres on the gravel drive went on for quite some time. Then all was silent while Ferne toyed with the man's nipple before her finger traced the contours of his powerful jaw. Her mood was quite subdued now, her body lying quietly in his arms. 'Will I make a good lover, Johnny?'

'I think you'll make a marvellous lover.'

'So will you teach me everything you know about sex?'

'Everything?'

'Absolutely everything.' She nodded into his neck and slid her hand over his shaft. 'I never do anything by halves. And, I'm a fast study.' She formed a coital ring between her thumb and fingers and worked his foreskin beguilingly, milking it of its pearly liquid.

Kissing her temple, he sighed and held her tighter. 'Yes – I can see you're a very fast learner.'

She nibbled at his ear. 'When can we have our next lesson?'

'Let's just get some sleep first, eh? I won't be any good for anything if you don't let me get my strength back.'

She squeezed him naughtily. 'How on earth did I ever have the luck to find a man like you?'

Chapter Three

FERNE FELT COLD when she awoke.

The open window fanned her with chilly morning air. But that was not the only reason for her coldness. Her hands searched in vain for the lover who had held her through the night.

He was gone. His cloak and boots were gone as well. Her own catsuit lay on the floor where he had peeled it off her, but her hood and mask still covered her head and face. Thank goodness he had not taken them off her while she'd slept.

Now she staggered into the bathroom, half hoping that he might be there. He wasn't. She groaned, held her head and looked blearily into the mirror. Was this the morning-after-the-night-before feeling which she had heard so much about?

Ferne showered quickly, the needles of water seeming to stimulate her breasts more than usual. As warm trickles spread over her stomach, they appeared purposefully to find their way between her legs, seeking out the secret lips which still felt sensitive, and which still desired to be touched.

She did touch them, but it was not the same feeling as his lips had created, nor the wonderful sensation of his tongue, or having that shaft of flesh parting them. That had been so exciting. At the first sight of it standing proudly, some primal instinct in her had made her want to bend and touch it. She had had a strange urge to take it in her mouth, and to feel it pulsing against her tongue.

Trying not to rub herself too hard, Ferne dried carefully, her skin still alive from his love-making. There was also that deep-seated ache she had felt for so long, and it seemed to be awakening again as her body came to life. She shrugged into a pair of designer jeans, buttoned up a pure white blouse and slipped a pink cashmere sweater over her shoulders, tying the sleeves around her neck. She would not wear a bra. As a newly liberated woman, she wanted to feel free. There was no way now that she was going to cage herself again.

Just as she was about to leave the bedroom, a sudden thought struck a dull note in her mind. She couldn't go down to breakfast if he was there. That would blow her cover. She thought of putting on the mask, but that was silly. As she stood pondering the dilemma, the clock in the tower struck loudly. She lost count and slumped on to the oak banquette by the window to gaze down on the courtyard of the castle. Bright sunshine lit the water of a fountain pool, sending little sparkles of light dancing over the pale blue coachwork of her Rolls Corniche. It stood alone where a dozen expensive cars had hemmed it tightly in the night before, barring her way should she have decided to escape.

Now she brightened. Was she the only one left? Of course, he might have come by taxi. No – he was not the type. A gigolo would drive a low, fast car. Had he seen her Rolls? If he had, he would know that she was well off. Damn. She should have brought her tubby little Micra town car. But what if he had gone? How would she contact him? How would they ever get to have sex again? Ferne decided to allow fate to take a hand.

A glance at the clock in the tower made her start. Twelve o'clock. Was it that late? She scampered down the sweeping stairs, stopping in horror at the ballroom where the revelry had taken over. It was a total mess.

Peeping cautiously around the door frame of the morning room, she found Lady Fanni Deighton-Smythe alone, gazing through the window which framed a view of verdant parkland.

Fanni spun around on hearing Ferne enter. 'Hello, darling. You're late. Did you oversleep?'

'I'm sorry. I . . .' Ferne blushed schoolgirlishly.

Fanni put up a dismissing hand. 'But you look absolutely radiant, darling. Did you have a good time last night?'

Ferne felt that the question was slightly loaded, but what the hell. Fanni would have soon put two and two together making an inspired five. 'Where is everybody?' Ferne was determined to keep up the pretence as long as she could get away with it.

Fanni waved a long cigarette holder dramatically

in the air. 'I fed them and pushed them all out hours ago. I can't bear people with hangovers milling about in the morning. And don't change the subject, Ferne Daville. Did you have somebody last night?'

'I "had" an interesting time.' Ferne kept it purposely short now, her guilt straining at her increasingly false air of nonchalance. But Fanni smiled an all-knowing smile, her dark eyes alight with the twinkle of a withheld secret.

'I've heard it called many things darling: exhilarating. Mindbending. But never "interesting".'

Ferne could not stop the blush which shot up her neck and filled her cheeks with a burning sensation. She needed to change the subject, but not too much. She needed data, not chat.

'Where did he go, Fan?'

Fanni gave her a raised eyebrow for an answer. 'Exactly which "he" are you referring to, darling?'

'Johnny, of course.' Ferne's hand went automatically to her mouth as Fanni's eyes filled with amusement.

'Not Johnny Stiff, by any chance?'

Ferne earnestly pretended ignorance but she knew that it didn't cover her confusion.

'They all have a Johnny Stiff, darling,' Fanni smirked. 'Now, if you describe it to me in great detail, I'll see if I can recognise it.'

Turning hurriedly to the breakfast buffet, Ferne fixed her attention pointedly on a bowl of cold scrambled egg and heaved. 'Do you want some toast, Fan?'

'Don't evade the issue, Ferne, dear. Whose prick did you take to bed with you last night?'

'Fanni. Really. You're impossible.' As she tried to spread a piece of crunchy toast with butter, Ferne's hand would not stop trembling.

'It's being "impossible" that makes life interesting, Ferne, darling. In your world of board meetings and power-wielding, I thought that you were a mistress of the art of being impossible. But we're getting off the subject. Just who did you have in your bed last night?'

Ferne resigned herself to the fact that if she was to renew her acquaintance with 'Johnny', she would have to come out in the open with Fanni. 'He was the Scots guy in the Batman outfit. You know – the tall one in the black hood and cape.'

'The one with that enormous horn under his tights?'

Again Ferne blushed. She took a deep breath to try to control it, but she knew that it came mostly from the flush of heat Fanni's description had released in her. 'Aren't they all like that?' Ferne said it with an air of studied innocence.

Fanni's smirk widened to a lascivious grin. 'Not all, darling. But even the smaller ones can be quite fun.'

Fern sat munching on her toast, glad of the small diversion. This was getting her nowhere and her anxiety was building by the minute. 'So who was the Scottish fellow in the Batman suit, Fan ? '

'The father of your baby, do you mean?' It was followed with a look of mock disapproval.

'You know I'm not so naïve as to get caught like that. Now – who the hell was he?'

Fanni made a pretence of thinking hard, but it didn't fool Ferne. 'I think he might have come with Alister McCrombie. Or was it Count Hauptenberg? I don't really know, darling. I just throw the parties. My victims come out of the woodwork for miles around to be here. Sorry I can't be more helpful, sweetie.'

The metallic blue Corniche whispered down the driveway. Ferne put out a hand and acknowledged Fanni as she stood on the drawbridge waving an enthusiastic goodbye.

With Ferne's mind whirring almost out of control, the journey back to Capthorne Beeches was fraught with a couple of near misses and a wrong turn. As she neared her country home, the ceaseless chatter of mental circuits gave way to deep depression. There was nothing to go home to but a large and rambling house, to servants she always had to show her best side to, and a pile of work a metre high which she had been persuaded to leave while she went to Fanni's for the weekend. Or was the depression because he'd gone without a goodbye? Now she began to feel used. But he had said that he would contact her with details of the plan to teach her the arts of sex. She just hoped that he would keep his word.

She turned the car into her driveway, the gilded iron gates swinging silently open in response to the built-in control in the car. A riot of roses and exotic shrubs swept past her side vision, giving way to the open parkland. The great timber and red-brick house built by prosperous ancestors loomed ahead, looking strangely grim. For the first time in her life, she was not happy to be back. She pulled up at the smaller Dower House where she had chosen to live alone unless she had guests.

The phone rang immediately she entered the front hall so that she had to dash to her study to catch it before it stopped.

'Hello, pussycat. Are you still purring?'

Ferne's stomach turned while her pulse began to race. And there was that thrill between her legs once more. The Scottish accent was soft and teasing, that thread of fun weaving through it again, making her solar plexus tighten.

'How did you get my number? It's ex-directory.' It was a silly outburst but it was all that came to mind.

Now there was a chuckle from the caller. She imagined the blue eyes shining. 'Fanni gave it to me. I called her this afternoon, but she wouldn't tell me your name or where you live. Is it some dark secret?'

Ferne's pulse raced wildly now. Thank goodness Fanni had kept her identity and address a secret. Above all, she must maintain her anonymity with this man. There was the chance of blackmail even if he did not make a bid for her affections in order to gain her wealth.

'So – how are you, Cleopatra?'

'I'm fine. But I miss you already.' It was blurted

out. Now, as he laughed, she felt silly. 'Can we meet?'

'Sorry, sweetheart. I'm calling from Scotland. I had to fly up to see a client today, otherwise I wouldn't have left you so early this morning.'

Immediately, Ferne felt jealous. Her mind filled in the naked details as it put up pictures of him working rhythmically over a slender, writhing young woman, her breasts lolling, her tongue out, his tight bottom heaving, and that prominent mole at the very tip of his spine clearly evident in her imagination.

Then she stopped her mind's erotic workings. His claim to be a gigolo had probably been a joke. 'You might have woken me to say goodbye this morning,' she pouted.

'I did say goodbye, but you didn't wake.'

'What do you mean?'

He chuckled again. 'I kissed you all over as you lay naked on the bed. I explored every inch of you with my tongue.'

'I don't believe you.'

'Believe whatever you like. Didn't you feel me when I sucked on your nipples? Even in your sleep they stood up hard.'

There had been a dream, and she had woken feeling randy, her nipples stiff, her vulval lips pleasantly engorged as they were engorging now. But she bristled. How dare he do that while she was asleep?

'I think you're an animal.'

A long, deep chuckle rippled down the phone

line. 'Of course I'm an animal. Why else do you like me? Was it not the animal in me you responded to last night?'

'Pig.'

'Cat.'

There came a long silence. Ferne was not sure if he was staying quiet with the purpose of keeping her dangling on a tense string. 'I thought you said you would teach me all about sex?'

'Aha. So you don't think me too much of a pig then?'

'Just shut up, will you? When can we meet?'

'Do I detect a note of desperation?'

'No you don't. I need you; that's all. You lit a fuse in me last night. Now if you don't do something to douse it, I'm sure I'll go off bang.'

'Oh dear.' Again, he chuckled.

She scowled. The man was a master of keeping her at the edge of stimulation. Then she took a deep breath, having to still her nerves. Even hearing his voice was sending shivers through her. They raced up to her neck and down again, curling under her, making her labia swell and throb.

'Tell me what's happening at your end, Cleopatra?'

It seemed strange to hear him call her that. She supposed she would get accustomed to it in time. 'I'm feeling very lonely and deserted.'

'Okay. Tell me what you want to do.'

'I told you. I want you. I want to learn all I can about . . .'

'Sex? Go on. Say it. Or are you too prudish?'

'Don't be ridiculous.'

'Then say it.'

'Sex. Sex. Sex. There – are you satisfied? Now, when are you going to teach me?'

'Are you really sure that's what you want?'

'Of course I'm damned well sure. I do know my own mind, you know.' Ferne was surprised at herself. She spoke sharply to employees but not usually to her friends. She put it down to the tension he was creating as she tried to pull a commitment from him. She wouldn't have had such trouble in her business dealings.

'All right. There's no need to snap my head off, Cleo.'

Cleo? That sounded nicer. It was much more intimate than Cleopatra. And nobody had ever coined a pet name for her before. Nobody had ever cared that much; except perhaps one man. And he had let her down. But that was long in the past. She thrust the painful memory aside.

'Sorry.' She fiddled with the phone cord, feeling sheepish.

'That's OK. What about the expenses? Can you afford me?'

'Look, there's no problem with money. Just tell me how much you want and I'll find it somehow.' She didn't tell him about the couple of million sterling she had in her personal account with nothing worthwhile to spend it on.

'OK. I can see you're a very independent lady. I think you should start your training as soon as possible.'

'Tonight?'

'Not tonight. I have an important engagement.'

'But I need you. I need to have you now, damn you.'

'I'm only sorry that you can't have me. But we can do the next best thing.'

'What the hell is that supposed to mean?'

'What are you doing with your hand?'

'I'm holding the damned phone, stupid.'

'And the other one?'

She went quiet. Her other hand was between her legs, the fingers running lightly over the tightness of her jeans. Was he a mind reader as well as a master of suspense?

'You're a devil. How did you know I was doing that?'

He laughed. 'It was just a good guess. Do you want to know what I'm doing with my free hand?'

'No I do not.'

'Are you sure?'

No, she wasn't sure. She wasn't sure of anything any more. This man had got her in a whirl. She had only known him for a few hours and he was making her do things, and feel things, and say things she would never have thought anyone could ever make her do.

'Put your hand inside your knickers.'

'I will not.'

'So – you are a prude, after all?'

'No I am not.'

'I thought you wanted to learn all about sex.'

'Not at the end of a blasted phone, I don't.'

'There are a lot of exciting things to do without touching one another, Cleo.' His voice was soft and pliant, but it didn't soften her.

'I don't care. I don't want to do it like this.'

'Are you telling me that you aren't getting excited?'

She was getting excited, damn him. Her finger had found its way into her jeans and she was sitting on the edge of her chair so that she could reach right into herself. And as he was crooning down the phone at her, the finger was working at her clitoris.

'All right. So I'm doing it. I hope you're satisfied.'

'You're wonderful – a bit naïve, but wonderful. You're a very good pupil. Now drop your knickers and put the phone between your legs.'

'Cut the damned wise cracks and tell me when I can meet you so we can do it properly.'

'Look, Cleo, the first thing you have to learn is to obey your tutor. If you can't accept that, that's fine by me. I'll put the phone down now.'

'No – don't.'

'All right, but if you want to learn about sex and love and bring out those feelings that you're caging, you'll have to let go a bit.'

'A bit? Hellfire, I'm a harlot compared with what I was this time yesterday.'

'Good. So you're a fast student. But we've hardly started. Now – do you want to know where and when to meet me?'

'Of course I do.'

'Then put the mouthpiece between your legs. I'll talk to you down there.'

'But that's blackmail.'

He laughed.

Ferne was shaking now. He was coercing her into doing things, knowing that, if she didn't, she would not get another sex session with him. Despite that, she did it. It was the wildest thing she had done yet. And he was working her into a slippery frenzy. He was a devil and he knew it. But she was learning fast. She needed to get it out of her system whatever it cost in money and in lost pride.

'Did you do it?'

'Just a damned minute. I can't get my knickers down.'

'Imagine me taking them down for you with my teeth. Feel my breath on your bush, my nose grazing your skin.'

She put the handset down on the desk and struggled with her jeans.

'Cleo? Don't you dare hang up on me.'

'Shut up. It isn't easy with one hand.' She thrust the handset down her panties, using it to slough them off. They dropped to her ankles where she stepped out of them.

'Widen your legs.'

She did.

'Now rub the phone gently through your pussy-lips.'

She rubbed the mouthpiece slowly between her legs, sliding it through her labia just as he had slid his shaft.

'I can't hear you, Cleo. Are you slippery?'

She was, and getting more so by the second. The sensations were turning her legs to jelly.'

'Rub me through your pussy again, Cleo. Pretend it's my tongue.'

She did rub it, and she felt so licentious. At first the plastic was cool on her secret lips, but as he spoke, there was the tiniest vibration which made her thrill out of all reason. She rubbed herself steadily, savouring each stroke, breathing deeply, unable to stop herself shaking.

'Mmmmmmm.' The small voice from between her legs was only just audible. It was like having him there. She could imagine his hot breath fanning on her sex, and the rasp of his tongue, then the wriggling tip of it pushing through her labia.

'Ahhh. That's wonderful, Cleo. Feel my mouth between the lips of your pussy.' There was a licking sound. He was breathing deeply as well, each pant making her more excited.

'Shall I tell you what I'm doing at my end?'

She didn't answer. She could imagine.

Now she increased the speed of her movement, opening her legs widely, bearing down on the handset in order to wring every last drop of sensation from it.

'I'm licking you again, Cleo. Can you feel me?'

Yes, she could. Lost in the lustfulness of the act, the small voice between her legs egged her on, stimulating her to a point of great tension. Her head went back, her mouth opened, her eyes closed tightly as she imagined that the sliding between her legs was the hot, strong shaft she had felt there last night. And now she knew that, in the absence of the real thing, this was probably the best thing he could do to relieve some of her tension.'

'Say it, Johnny. Say the word.' She shouted it so that the microphone would pick it up.

'Fuck, Cleo. I want to fuck you.' It came muted from the handset, but it set her alight. Frantically she rubbed herself with the phone, whispering the word to every stroke. And then she came, letting out a deep-seated moan.

'Ahhhh.' The sound came up from her parted legs, just as if he were down there, ejaculating with her, in her and over her. And she continued to rub herself gently, keeping the rhythm of her small contractions going for as long as she could make them. When finally they stopped, she raised the handset to her mouth, smelling her scent strongly on the plastic.

'Animal.'

'Grrrr. But did you like it?'

'Mmmmmmm. But I'd rather it had been live.'

'Can you be in London tomorrow?'

'When?' It took Ferne by surprise. She knew that she had a full diary. It was a particularly difficult time to begin an adventure like this. But then she told herself that she had not taken a holiday for a while, and anyway, there were others in her organisation who would have to earn their fat salaries for once. Let them take some of the strain. It might be good for them.

'I could make it at four.'

'Three-thirty, or nothing.'

Normally she would have said no. She expected people to fall in with her plans and did not let others make her schedules. But this was different. This was something she could not control. If she did try to, she was sure that it would not work.

'I'll make it at three-thirty. What shall I wear?' Again, she would never normally ask anyone that; especially not a man. But she wanted to get this right. It was important.

'Wear whatever you like, sweetheart. You'll soon be naked, so it doesn't matter very much.'

The idea of having him strip her again made her stomach do a little roll. Her solar plexus fluttered and her clitoris began to come alive once more. She whispered' 'What are we going to do, Johnny? Tell me so I can prepare myself.'

'I'll set out a programme of tuition for you. It'll take you on a journey of discovery you'll never forget. Just leave it until tomorrow, eh?'

'All right.' She knew that her disappointment sounded in her voice, but there was nothing she could do to stop it now. 'How much money should I bring?'

'Ten thousand pounds.'

'But I didn't think it would be . . .'

'I thought you said you wanted the best. You do want to experience everything, don't you?'

'I do, but I . . .'

'Can't you raise that much?'

'I'll try. But . . .'

'No buts, Cleo. That's the deal. Ten thousand pounds up front and you get everything.'

'Everything?'

'The best tuition money can buy. I promise I won't cheat you. And you'll never be the same again.'

'Do I have any choice?'

'Of course you do. You can put the phone down now.' He was clearly a hard negotiator; just like she normally was herself. It was strange to be on the other end of a deal that she could not control. He had her just where he wanted her, but not where she wanted him. Damn. Perhaps she should pull out. But, although her common sense was hammering hard inside her head, her body was fighting back. It was so desperate to feel him just once more.

'I'll come. Where?' She nervously scribbled the address he gave her. 'I'll be there. But there is one thing, Johnny. I want to wear a mask.'

There was a long silence. She could imagine him frowning.

Then the cheerful voice came again. 'Whatever you want, lassie. This is your coming-out party.'

Ferne looked out across the City of London far below her top-floor office. Then she swung her chair around angrily. 'Look, Robert, I can't help it. I've just got a more important meeting to attend, that's all.' She glared at her senior director across the deeply polished rosewood of her desk.

Robert Trenchard looked down upon her coolly.

The old man had known her since she was born and he never rose to her taunts or reacted to her tempers. He was more like a father to her than her father had been. As her most trusted colleague, he was indispensable.

'But we have to see the Board of Van Hagen Industries this afternoon, Miss Ferne. They're proving to be more awkward than I'd hoped.'

'What exactly is the problem, Robert?'

'Essentially, they want to run their own show. As you know, Mr Van Hagen is a very independent man. Your father had trouble with him. And now it seems that he doesn't like being dictated to by a . . .' The grey eyes scanned her warily.

'By a jumped-up stripling of a woman?' Ferne finished the remark for him. She knew it well. Ever since she had taken the reins of Daville Holdings, she had had this attitude from people. But she was fast on her feet, and had degrees in economics and business management which stood her in good stead. And she was a very fast learner. Since the age of fifteen, her father had trained and groomed her to take the Chair of the Board of Daville when he died.

'Mr Van Hagen didn't complain when we funded development of his new plastics material, Robert. Without our support, he would have got nowhere. Other City investors wouldn't look at it.'

'But Hagenite could make us all a great deal of money, Ferne. Its properties are unique. There's an enormous commercial potential as well as the military market. We would have a world monopoly for several years.'

'Then what's old man Van Hagen grouching about?'

'It isn't the old man, Ferne. He's taking a back seat to his son Jan now. I thought you knew that.'

Ferne went cold. Yes, she knew that Jan Van Hagen was back from the States and had taken the reins on the Hagenite development. He'd called her several times. He had pestered her for a dinner-date and she had resisted him. Her hurt at his desertion of her seven years earlier still stung her more deeply than she dared to let herself feel.

'What the hell does Jan Van Hagen think we are, Bob? We've sunk three and a half million into Hagenite so far. We must have a controlling say in the running of the business.'

'Young Van Hagen's very grateful for our support, but he still thinks he can run his own show. I suppose I would think the same if I was a Harvard business graduate.'

'Nonsense. The man's a self-opinionated pig.'

Ferne swivelled angrily in her chair. She could do without this kind of hassle today; especially from Jan Van Hagen. She was tense; her body still alive with the libido which the 'telephone' liaison with Johnny had created the night before. Even though she had orgasmed, it had not been that avalanche of energy pouring over her that his real love-making had produced. She just hoped that that wouldn't prove to have been the pinnacle of her sexual experience. Now she was faced with the problems which running a multi-million-pound, international business created. No wonder she had never had time for sex.

'How much do we own in Van Hagen Enterprises, Robert?

'Forty-three per cent of their stock.'

She chewed her pen. 'And they hold the other fifty-seven?'

He shook his head. 'Van Hagen owns forty-three per cent too. The other fourteen per cent is held elsewhere.'

'Where exactly?' She was alert now to the possibility of gaining control of Van Hagen Enterprises over the head of her former fiancé. If they had been foolish enough not to keep a majority holding of their stock, she'd teach Jan Van Hagen a lesson in business if not in humility.

Trenchard rubbed his chin thoughtfully. 'I don't know exactly who owns the remaining stock, Ferne. A number of small shareholders, I think. The Institutions wouldn't look at it. Too risky.'

'Then I want you to find the floating shares and buy a controlling interest. Once we have that, we'll soon see who calls the tune. And I'll have Van Hagen by the balls,' she whispered to herself.

'But, Ferne, I don't th—'

She put up a pre-emptive hand. 'Just do it, Bob. I'll see you in the morning. You can debrief me about the meeting with Van Hagen then.'

The address Johnny had given Ferne led her to a large front door in the centre of an elegant Edwardian terrace, four storeys high and with a basement below. Geraniums framed the black door with scarlet and white, the brass knocker and letter plate shining as brightly as the day they had been screwed to the red brick wall.

In the hot afternoon sunshine, Ferne climbed the steps lightly, the jeans and shirt she had worn seeming out of place here.

At exactly three-thirty her finger pressed the brass bell-push decisively. There was no reason to be timid. She knew what she had come for and that was all there was to it. To hell with what anyone else thought.

The door swung open silently. Ferne expected to see the mischievous face of Johnny and was taken aback to find herself looking into the dark, slanting eyes of a beautiful, oriental young woman. The woman smiled openly and beckoned her in.

Ferne stepped over the threshold demurely. She had not expected to be met by a servant. But that was not unusual. All Fanni's party-goers were well off. She would never invite anyone who was otherwise.

'I've come to see Mr . . .' Her heart fluttered. She didn't know anything but his fictitious name.

'Mister Johnny told me to expect you, Miss Cleopatra. Please come in.' It was a soft and lilting voice, and it went with the softly moulded features. The young woman was tall and slender, her face oval, her skin as clear as a baby's, honey brown with just a tint of coffee in the hollows.

Ferne followed obediently, pleasantly impressed by the quiet opulence of the hallway. The ambience was one of restrained good taste. Antique pieces graced the space, crowned with wonderful oriental vases. The walls were hung with vibrant watercolours of mountains, lakes and forests.

'My name is Mai Lin.' The woman bowed slightly and gestured to Ferne to follow her into a sitting-room, similarly furnished to the entrance hall. As Ferne studied more paintings, more translucent porcelain, and the intricately inlaid woodwork of the furniture, her feet sank into a Chinese silk carpet. In its sculpted contours, red dragons chased blue birds with long and flowing tail feathers.

Ferne was startled as she looked up to find the black eyes studying her closely. She smiled as Mai Lin handed her an envelope, while making another little bow. 'For you.'

With shaking fingers Ferne slit the envelope open quickly, revealing two sheets of paper. The first was ivory-coloured vellum, written in a flowing hand. *Welcome to the revelation of your sensuality. The course will consist of five lessons and will be an adventure full of erotic wonder and tenderness which I hope you will never forget for the whole of your lifetime. Johnny.*

Below that was written: *Lesson One. Getting to Know Your Man.*

Ferne felt demure as she folded the first sheet and looked at the second. It was clearly an invoice for ten thousand pounds. What the hell. In her world you paid for what you expected to get, so why should this be so different? Turning to Mai Lin, Ferne smiled thinly. 'Will you take a personal cheque, made out to cash?'

The little bow told her yes, and she quickly wrote a cheque for the whole amount on a blank form she'd collected from her bank. God help Johnny if he didn't deliver.

'Please come this way, Miss Cleopatra.' Mai Lin bowed and gestured towards a door. Just as she opened it for Ferne to go through, she whispered, 'But did you not want to wear your mask?'

Ferne's heart nearly stopped. She had forgotten all about her anonymity. She doubted that being seen by Mai Lin would matter. It was only important that Johnny didn't see her face.

She had taken her hair up in the manner of Brigitte Bardot – sex-kitten style – and she thought how well it suited her. It certainly suited her mood. As the preliminaries had progressed, she had become more and more impatient.

Slipping a half-mask out of her shoulder bag, she put it on, sighting herself in an ornately framed mirror. Good. It just covered her eyes, half of her forehead, and left the bridge of her nose free. She had wanted to wear the hood from the catsuit but that had been left at Fanni's and she could hardly have gone back and asked for it without inviting a cascade of awkward questions. So this small mask would have to do. No one would recognise her easily.

Mai Lin smiled as she ushered Ferne through the doorway. Before she knew what was happening, there was a click of the lock behind her. Ferne's heart sped like a car engine revving, the driver keyed up for the start of a great contest.

The room was not large, but neither was it cramped. The silky furnishings in soft pastel shades endowed it with a muted feel, the closed curtains and the carpets pink and blue and gold. A large bed covered with a sheet of pink material seemed to shimmer in the glow of wall lamps, the light defused and tinged with rose. It gave the room a feeling of sensual warmth.

Gilt-framed mirrors around the walls and over the bed reflected the silk from different angles. Ferne trembled at the thought of lying there naked, watching her reflections as Johnny and she made love. But where was Johnny?

For a moment Ferne stood tentatively, her many reflections making it appear that there were several kittenish young women waiting to be loved. Should she undress? Should she prepare herself for when he arrived to take her? No; she would not be so forward. Part of the tension would be gained from letting him undress her, just as she had let him strip her of the catsuit, lap between her legs and suckle on her breasts.

Then she heard a sound. At first she thought it was a fan, but she quickly realised that it was humming; melodious and soft. It came from a door in the corner, slightly ajar and showing a thin strip of light. A bathroom?

Ferne set her shoulder bag and the letter on the bed. With legs trembling, she used her fingers to widen the gap in the doorway until light flooded through. A stream of air rushed out, bearing invigorating freshness of the kind that comes with the torrential rains after a thunderstorm. She breathed in deeply and braced herself, half expecting to find Johnny soaking in the bath.

A black-masked, blond-haired man, naked to the waist, looked up and smiled as he said, 'Hello.' As he turned to her fully, sapphire blue eyes flashed in amusement, catching her own eyes and fixing them, making her take a deeper breath. Then he gave a face-wide smile, his teeth flashing brightly in the bathroom lights.

Ferne sighed with pleasure. The softness of his Scottish accent on the word 'hello' brought back a flood of memories of their first encounter.

Light reflected from his hair, shining like spun gold. His skin glowed with a patina of radiant health. And the strong and slender hands which had worked between her legs rested on his hips. The hips bore elegantly cut denim jeans, tight enough to show a prominent bulge containing something which made Ferne's solar plexus thrill. She had an almost irresistible urge to touch it.

At Fanni's she had only seen him in the moonlight, and mostly in dark shadow. He was beautiful, the face masculine but kind, the torso tight, undulating with the confirmation of well-developed muscles. He was slimmer than she remembered him through the champagne daze. And he was also younger than she'd thought. She put his age at twenty-two at most. That was far younger than his voice had told her, and younger than the picture her mind had conjured for her since that pulsing entanglement of limbs and breasts and sexual parts.

'Hello.' She lowered her gaze for a second, feeling awed before this Adonis. But he was her own Adonis. This seemed to set every nerve fibre of her body alight, and the secret place between her legs was already an inferno of heat and sensual pleasure.

She closed her eyes as he brushed his fingers admiringly through her hair. Then she fixed his eyes with feigned confidence and threw back her head. 'What are we going to do?'

He put his finger to his mouth, indicating that he wanted silence. She realised that chattering might have broken the spell for both of them.

Ferne found herself drawn to him. She was being pulled by her need to touch him, to have him touch her, and to experience him as fully as it was possible for a woman to experience any man. Now, as she ventured close, he put his arms around her and took her to himself, the warmth of his neck on her cheek, her lips kissing at his powerful shoulder. A spicy scent wafted to her nose, rushing through her head.

She lowered her hand and ran it over his shaft, cupped his balls, and closed her eyes. My God, she wanted this man more than she wanted anything in the world right now.

Chapter Four

FERNE HELD HERSELF against the man's tautness for several minutes, just sensing him – his breathing, his heat, and the blend of spice and musk of his scent. And she rubbed his penis lightly with her palm, feeling how it stiffened at her touch.

Her stomach rose and fell against his, each of his rises matching her falls.

He did nothing but hold there as the fingertips of her other hand roved lightly over his back, feeling the smoothness of his skin.

'Shall we go next door?' Even though whispered, her words sounded as loud as a public announcement in the stillness of the bathroom, only his gentle breathing and the dull thump of her heart audible before.

'Okay.' As he whispered it softly into her ear there was a lightness in his tone that she had not heard before. He sounded much younger. But that could have been her memory playing tricks. Her original impressions had been forged under the effects of her intoxication by both him and the champagne.

Ferne led him by the fingertips to the bedroom, walking backwards so that she didn't have to take her eyes off him. And now they stood with his back to the bed, the spicy aftershave evoked scenes of a tropical beach: white sands and tall palms; azure skies with racing clouds; and a rampant, naked young man chasing her through the surf.

The soft light gave a glow to his skin as she watched his back in several mirrors. The jeans, tight around his behind, enabled her to see the cheeks fully defined, the legs long and straight, slightly apart as he held her against him.

She wanted to see that bottom naked. There had always been something about men's bottoms that had stirred her, even though she had admonished herself each time. But now she did not need any self-admonishment. As she undressed him, she would touch him and experience him with her tongue and lips. She would explore him fully and let him explore every inch of her.

'Lover?'

'Yes, Cleopatra?'

'What do you want to do?'

He leaned down and picked up the paper from the bed and she scanned it sideways. *Getting to know your man.*

'But how can I get to know you like this?'

He let out a small breath of amusement which fanned her temple before he let a little kiss settle delicately on her forehead. This seemed so different from the way he had behaved before. He was just being there, doing nothing, making no move to take her. Was he expecting her to do all the work? Was she to explore him?

Ferne traced the hard line of his collar-bone, moving to the hollow notch under his strong neck, and down the deep groove between his breasts. They were such muscular breasts that they hardly gave under her fingers as she moved across them, her middle finger working little circles until it found the small but prominent nipples. Something in her made her lick the finger before encircling the nipple around and around until it stood as proud as she could make it.

'That's nice.' He stroked her back and then guided her away from him and downwards until her mouth found the nipple and sucked on it gently.

'Mmmm.'

Encouraged by his response, she set a line of sucking kisses across the valley of his breastbone until she found the other little stud already standing proud.

'Is that nice?'

'Mmmmm.' He threw his head back and closed his eyes.

As she bit his waist, he raised his head and growled in the back of his throat.

She thrilled at the response, her already engorged secret lips throbbing with the excitement the animalistic sound transmitted. But she would not evoke his passion to take her yet. She would titillate him just as he had titillated her when he had slid his shaft through her labia and she had desperately tried to capture it within herself.

She lapped him, feeling the smoothness of his hairless chest, travelling downwards until she found his navel with the wisp of golden hair spiralling around it. The tip of her tongue probed deeply, tasting saltiness before moving on.

Now she was on her knees before him, her arms around his buttocks, her cheek pressed to the bulge in his trousers. She felt him stir, and instantly needed to bare his cock. She needed to see it, to scent it, and to hold it naked in her hand.

With her fingers trembling and a series of small contractions opening and closing her secret lips, she undid the buckle at his waist. She could hardly hold the zip tab as her fingers trembled at her boldness. No childhood Christmas parcel had ever contained the excitement that this unwrapping held. No twenty-first birthday surprise – no matter how expectant of heavy gold or diamonds – could match the tense anticipation of exposing that which lay within his trousers. It was a gift he was allowing her to unwrap on her voyage of discovery.

Ferne was surprised at the length of it when she peeled aside his fly and revealed the pinky helmet of her prize. It was already almost up to his waistband, and far longer than she recalled. And now as she ran her fingers down its length, she felt it hard and curving.

'Mmmm.' He set back his head and thrust towards her.

Putting her lips to the head, she closed her eyes and breathed his aroma. It set up a curious pressure in her forehead, which seemed to send pulses of excitement to her breasts and the tight skin of her loins.

The highly profiled shape of the helmet felt so smooth to her pursed lips. It had the silkiness of fine velvet, warm and tongue-inviting.

Her tongue came out to probe the groove of the head, the small web of skin stretched tightly. And when she ran the tip of her tongue downwards, the whole helmet swelled and became shiny with the pressure within it. It lost its delicate pinkness, becoming more plum-coloured, its form even more pronounced.

Slowly she peeled him, her tongue exploring, lapping every millimetre of his flesh.

The jeans dropped away now. He let her remove them completely, taking up a legs-wide stance again, hands on his hips, his face smiling down at her.

She looked upwards for a moment, up along the curving shaft, over its bulging glans, the taut, strong stomach, through the deep valley of his chest, scanning the smiling mouth and finding his penetrating eyes. The smile flashed wider as he whispered, 'Don't stop now.'

And so her hands ran over his tight buttocks as her lips pressed to his shaft. Now she buried her nose in the wrinkled pouch which held his testes. Her tongue came out and licked a small seam of skin which made the pouch appear to be two halves sewn together. As she traced it with her tongue, the shaft hardened more, making springing movements under her cat-lick touch.

Again, he set back his head and thrust his pelvis forward, forcing her into harder contact with the object of her exploration.

She wanted to feel it deep inside her again, thrusting and working until she exploded with the delight it brought. And she wanted to feel that flush of heat as he pumped into her, and to hear him groan with pleasure, his hot chest pressing her breasts so tightly that she almost squealed with the delight of it.

But she would wait.

She would explore him. After all, this was her first practical lesson in the male anatomy.

Ferne tore off her blouse, baring her breasts to him. They swelled out with the tension in her body. She lay on the floor and pulled off her jeans, baring her sex to him as she stripped her panties off. With her legs wide open, she showed herself to him, warm and succulent, and she thrilled at the wantonness of the act.

As he moved to stand over her, she reached up to lap at his pouch. She was mesmerised as his testes retracted from her tongue and the shaft juddered with the reaction.

She licked the inside of his thighs, just as he had licked hers. And she ran kisses over his groin and up to his navel again. Here she found the shaft trapped between her chest and the underside of her chin.

She rose, her breasts working up his thighs before enclosing his shaft in their deep valley. Then she pressed her breasts together around it, working it down through her cleavage so that the hood of skin came up over the head before she plunged down again, stripping the plummy helmet, making it stretched and shiny as it emerged once more.

Now she took it in her hand, gliding the foreskin up and down. It was so mobile and so smooth that it slid like silk over the head. With each stroke he let out a little moan of pleasure.

'Is that nice?'

'Mmmm. Wonderful.'

Ferne smiled at the compliment. Whoever would have thought that she'd be kneeling under a gorgeous man, working his shaft so delicately when she should have been engaged in a boardroom battle with Van Hagen.

As she rose and stood close, she felt his hardness against her pubis, his stomach on hers, his chest undulating against her breasts and his mouth against her own. She opened her legs, trying to mirror his stance, trying to feel the shaft just sliding across her clitoris, too high to enter her unless she stood upon tiptoe or he bent his knees to accommodate the difference in their heights.

He seemed taller than she remembered. He was willowy yet strong, hard yet smooth – so utterly masculine.

As she bit into the junction of his shoulder and his neck, she let out a low growl from the back of her throat. She was being a she-cat, and she was loving every second of it.

She bit again and scored his back with her nails. He shuddered and thrust himself hard against her pubis.

In the mirrors as she watched her hands working lovingly at first, then clawing, she felt wild and abandoned, a female animal on heat, yearning to be mated.

It was such a strong back, without an ounce of spare flesh. Now she could view the reflection of that tight-muscled bottom, the sides deeply dimpled in while the mounds were firm and rounded.

Completely uniform in colour, his skin was the shade of honey with no white marks of swimwear to mar it. There was not a mark on him to spoil anything at all.

He began to spring now, working himself against her bush of hair. Each spring took him on an upward stroke, tightening her pubic skin which in turn tightened her clitoris. She wanted to widen to him so that she could contact him fully and get the stimulation her swollen little nub needed for its satisfaction.

As she watched him working, the muscles of his thighs flexed, the calves locked in a line of tense tissue which stood out proudly. My God, he was so strong, so raunchy, and so marvellously sexual. He was a prime example of his species and she deserved him.

She deserved him because she was beautiful too, but in an entirely different way. She had known since adolescence that she was a sensuous creature and she had used it to influence men, even though she had not encouraged them openly. In fact, each time they responded to her subtle body movements – those little looks she shot them, those small pouts of her lips – she would freeze them out. They would either cower with their sexual tails between their legs or they would become angry. Then, as cool as ice, she would admonish them for their tempers and instil the idea that if they behaved themselves they might just please her. And if they pleased her, she would allow them to believe that they might possess her too.

Was this the power she wielded? Was it nothing to do with her intellect, her lightning-quick mind, her sharp grasp of the essence of every argument, deal or proposal? Whatever it was, she had been successful at it. She had learned to be a manipulator of the male in the boardroom, now she was learning how to manipulate him in the bedroom. And by the moans and the sighs and the little pumping movements in his organ, she judged that she was learning well.

Kneeling between his legs, she held him around the thighs, her mouth kissing at the top of the plummy helmet. Her lips circled around it, feeling the prominent ridge where it sat upon the shaft.

She closed her eyes.

Slowly she slid him into her mouth, savouring every inch. Now she could feel veins throbbing against her tongue. She drove downwards until the pulsing head reached the back of her throat, her top lip grazing his mat of golden hair, her nose pressing deep into the area just above his pubic bone. She knew from her own feelings how painfully sensual this could be.

'Ahhh. That's wonderful,' he whispered.

She sucked harder.

He groaned, thrusting into her mouth, his hands around the back of her scalp, pulling her on to himself.

In response she began to work slowly, sucking up his foreskin and plunging down once more. She was warmly wet with the excitement she was creating in herself, and the walls of her vagina were contracting hard. Quite involuntarily they clamped and then released, yearning to have something to clamp on.

Now his pelvis was thrust forwards, his legs frogged outwards, his stomach drawn in, and his head thrown back. It was just the way her body had reacted as he had sucked between her legs on their first encounter.

'Ahhh. Ohhh, my God,' he moaned as she mouthed him.

Now she sat back on her haunches, and she worked him with one hand, pushing her fingers hard into his stomach between his navel and his pubis.

She worked him steadily and sensuously, milking the rearing shaft just as she had milked cows on the home farm as a child. And when he came it was like a tidal bore. It rose under her hand from the root of his shaft, fountaining with great force.

As he spurted, she came in sympathy. Not in an explosion, but in an unstoppable flush, her tension rising slowly until it overflowed in delightful waves and small contractions.

Instinctively she pressed herself to it to let it pump against her neck. It beat in her hand, his breath gasping, his stomach heaving. Against her cheek it was slippery and alive. Her tongue came out and licked its head. She lapped it as if it were a pulsing lollipop, tasting the saltiness of his semen, revelling in the ecstasy of having made him climax.

He sank to the bed, his arms above his head, his legs open, and his feet planted firmly on the floor. She sank with him, not letting go of him for a second.

With his legs wide spread, her hands working at his nipples, she lapped his stomach. Then she licked his shaft. And she licked his pouch, with the testes hanging loosely now, and she lapped around the hollows of his loins. With her tongue and lips she experienced the most intimate moments of a man's pleasure, focussing all his attention on the one thing which he prized above all others.

Ferne judged that when a woman did this to a man, he might become addicted to her. He would become compliant to her will and a willing subject under the sensuous workings of her mouth. He would give himself up to her and lie back like this man was lying back, being administered to and having every millimetre of his sexuality admired.

Ferne felt pleasantly tired. The energy expended

in her ministrations plus that spent in her own climax had left her relaxed. She floated within a haze of softness as she knelt between his legs, suckling the softening organ tenderly, her cheek against his groin.

And so she dozed.

How long she slept, Ferne did not know. But when she awoke, she was alone. She sat up with a start.

Naked, she tiptoed to the bathroom, fully confident of finding Johnny in the shower. She would join him, soap him, caress him and make him take her hard. It was her turn now.

The disappointment of the empty bathroom was hurtful. Sadness was its main component, mixed with a tinge of annoyance. She had not finished and now he had done to her exactly what he'd done before. He'd left her asleep and crept away – back into someone else's bed, no doubt.

Without bothering to shower, she tugged on her clothes and stormed out of the door, ripping off the mask as she went.

In the salon Mai Lin sat, her eyes bright and welcoming as she looked up from a book.

'Where is he? I want to see him now.'

Mai Lin rose sedately and smiled enigmatically, her dark eyes alight with amusement.

'I am sorry, Miss Cleopatra, but the lesson is over. Was it a good lesson?'

Yes, it had been good. It had been better and more rewarding than she could have hoped for.

But now she was strung out. She wanted more. And she would not stand for being dumped every time he had had enough of her. Damn him. Who the hell did he think he was, giving her the runaround?

'You didn't answer me, Mai Lin. Where's Johnny?'

A small query showed in the other woman's eyes, then she reached for an envelope from a side table.

'Mr Johnny asked me to give you this after your lesson. Please open it.'

Ferne's hands trembled with annoyance this time as she tore the envelope apart.

Congratulations on the completion of your first tutorial. I hope that you found it interesting.

Ferne snorted. She had used the word 'interesting' to Fanni. Now she understood how entirely impotent it was in the context of the afternoon's experience. It had been far more than interesting. It had been fascinating and addictive.

She set her head proudly and read the remainder of the letter. *And I wish you success in Lesson Two: Getting to know yourself.*

Ferne snapped her eyes on to the oriental beauty. Mai Lin watched her quietly in response.

'When am I supposed to come again, Mai Lin?'

'I do not know, Miss Cleopatra. Mr Johnny will call you.'

And to Ferne's surprise Mai Lin took her by the hands, kissed her fully on the lips and led her to the door.

Ferne stormed into the Dower House after seven o'clock that evening, her body alight with annoyance mixed with a tension which came from unrequited sexual need. Although she had come to a climax, it seemed that she needed to feel a man inside her for there to be that explosive release of energy she had felt the first time.

She usually only came down to Capthorne Beeches at the weekends, but there were important arrangements to be made for guests this week. Now she stomped around the kitchen, angrily pushing buttons on the microwave oven. And she swore loudly and repeatedly.

'Damned arrogant pig. Just you wait until I get my hands on your balls again, mister. I'll teach you to walk out on me before I've finished with you.'

She ate the casserole her cook had left, and gulped a glass of mineral water. As time had gone on, doubts about her sanity had been forming. What had she done? She had started on a slippery slope which had no hand-holds and she felt out of control. On the one hand she wanted to pull out of the deal now. No one did this to her and got away with it. But on the other hand her body was already hooked on the energies which coursed through it. She knew that if he did telephone her, she would have a hard time stopping herself melting to that sexy, fun-filled voice.

That was something which still puzzled her. His voice had been lighter somehow – not so resonant.

He had said very little during their encounter; just a few words of encouragement and those *ahh's* and *oh's* which had set her tingling, knowing that she was creating feelings that he could not contain. He had looked younger than she had remembered him to be. And there had been something else about him which she could not quite put her finger on. She smiled at her mental pun and closed her fingers as if closing on that throbbing shaft. It had seemed longer and more whippy; not the strong, thick stem of flesh she had felt deep inside her at Fanni's. But then, she had not held it on their first night. She had not even touched it, and in the dimness of the castle bedroom, who knew what tricks the light had played?

But, all in all, it had been a fulfilling experience even though she was still as frustrated as a caged-up cat on heat.

He didn't ring.

Ferne paced the floor all evening, unable to deal with important correspondence, unwilling to go out in the grounds to walk off her energy in case he did call. By midnight she was a time-bomb ready to blow. She was out of control for the first time in her life. She had no line on him, no way of finding him and making him take her. She doubted that he'd respond to her demand anyway; he seemed too independent a kind of guy. So she had paid out thousands and had no way of calling it back if they'd been clever and taken it straight round to her bank. Her cheque made out to cash was too liquid to have any control over as soon as it had left her hands. It was as good as gold. And she would not forfeit that amount of money by pulling out of the deal. Her only course of action was to go through with the next lesson at least. That way she could grab him and screw a name out of him if nothing else, or she would have no recourse to justice if he decided to cut and run with her money. She'd been a fool to pay it all at once.

Damn.

When the phone by Ferne's bed rang, the clock read one o'clock. She had not been able to sleep. She snatched it up and put on the light.

'Yes. Who's this?'

'Hey, pussycat, draw your claws in, and stop bristling your fur, will you?'

'Why the hell did you walk out on me?'

'Shhh. Calm down and tell me what's eating you. Didn't you have a good time this afternoon?'

'You know damned well I did. Then you sneaked out, just as you did at Fanni's.'

'You sound frustrated.'

'Of course I'm bloody well frustrated. What the hell do you expect when you let me work myself up and then leave before I can come?'

'Was that what happened?'

'You know damned well it was.'

'But the lesson was one of exploration, lassie. It was to help you learn what makes a man tick.' He laughed.

'Stop making fun of me, Johnny. You can't get me all keyed up and then not – then not . . .'

'Then not screw you, do you mean?'

'Yes, that's exactly what I mean.'

'Sorry. But I told you; we must take this a few easy steps at a time.'

'I don't recall you wanting to take any "easy steps" at Fanni's. All you wanted was to get in my knickers as fast as you could.'

'That was different.'

'How was it different?'

'This is a business arrangement. Getting in your knickers comes later.'

'There won't be any later if you keep running out on me. I won't come again.'

'Not with me, you won't.' He laughed again. 'But that's entirely your prerogative.'

'I'll want a refund.'

Now he chuckled loudly. 'There's no chance of that, sweetheart. Consider your money spent. Now – if you want to chicken out and forfeit my fee, be my guest.'

'Oh no. You don't get my money that easily. I'll screw every last penny out of you before I've finished.'

As he laughed loudly, she realised her gaff. Damn again.

'Look, pussycat – you asked me to help you experience sex in all its forms. I said I'd help. If it's a bit painful, I'm sorry; but that's just how it is. If you've played at being a nun until the age of twenty-five, don't blame me. Now – what are we going to do about this frustration?'

'You're going to come round here and . . .' She stopped herself. That was the last thing she wanted him to do. Once he knew where she lived he would find out who she was and then things would change. It was vital to keep her identity a secret from him.

'I'm not going to come round there and do anything, sweetheart. I'm speaking to you from Scotland, so I'm afraid it's impossible. I could give you a number to ring if that's what you want. I can guarantee whoever comes will be good. And very discreet.'

'You must be mad. What would I want with a . . .'

'With a gigolo?'

As he laughed loudly again Ferne knew that she had been trapped. But what was it about this man that kept her at his command the whole time?

'Are you still there, pussycat?' The tone was caring – wooing even. It brought back the sensation of tenderness she had experienced with him.

'Yes, I'm still here, though I ought to put down the phone on you.'

'Why?'

'Because you've got me in a spin, that's why.' She didn't know why she was telling him, but she was. She needed to have him there, on her phone even if she couldn't have him in any other way. She needed to hear his voice and to be told how beautiful she was. Somehow it mattered to her what he thought of her, and she was not putting up a very good impression.

'I'm sorry, Johnny. I'm all worked up. You know what I need and I can't get it.'

'Sorry. I don't like to hear you like this.'

'Do you really care?'

'Of course I care. I don't just jump into bed with anyone, you know. I told you, I'm very discerning.'

'I don't believe you.'

'Believe what you like. But don't take your frustration out on me. It's time to grow up, Cleo. Now – can we start afresh?'

She let out a long sigh. 'I suppose so.'

He whispered. 'Are you in bed?'

'Yes.'

'And how are you dressed?'

'In a negligee.'

'Is the light on?'

'Yes.'

'Good. Now take off the negligee.'

She obeyed, her body trilling again to his wooing tone.

'Can you see yourself in a mirror?'

She could, and she kicked aside the duvet and opened her legs to show herself her swollen sex just as she'd showed him that afternoon as she'd lain on the floor.

'Now kiss me, Cleo.'

'How the h—?'

'Just put the phone to your lips and kiss me.'

She did it, closing her eyes, imagining his smiling lips.

'You're very beautiful, Cleo. Has anyone ever told you that?'

'Not in as many words,' she whispered as she scanned her supine body in the mirror.

'You have a wonderful smile and gorgeous eyes.

I didn't see your hair but I presume it's black.'

'How could you know that?'

'By your pussy, of course.'

She ran her hand over her mound, recreating the feeling of him kissing her there.

'Let me feel your breasts.'

She rubbed the phone over her nipples one by one.

'That's marvellous. Now, are you feeling more relaxed?'

'I suppose so. But when can we do this for real, Johnny?'

'We will, sweetheart. Soon.'

'Make it really soon. I need you.'

'Be patient.'

'Can I come tomorrow?'

'I can't see you tomorrow.'

'But you must. I can't hold out for long. I'll go up the wall.'

'I'll arrange your next lesson and let you know when and where.'

'Soon?'

'All right. Now, put me between your legs and let me talk to your pussy.'

'She opened her legs wide, bent her knees up and rubbed the phone slowly over herself, watching in the mirror on her dressing-table.

'Hello, pussy.' It was very faint. 'I just want to say how wonderful I think you are.'

She smiled and slid the phone through her well lubricated labia.

'You're so warm and tender. And so succulent. I

adore the way you open and shut on me.'

Ferne put back her head and sighed.

'And I want you to know that I'll fuck you nicely as soon as I possibly can. So be patient, pussy. Be patient.'

Ferne's heart was racing now. Her stroke was getting faster and she was panting. This was crazy but it was wracking her up again.

'Mmmmm. That's nice, Cleo, but I've got to go.'

'Johnny? Johnny, don't ring off.'

'It's late, Cleo. I have an important meeting in the morning.'

'But—'

'Shhhh, my love. Just kiss me and go to sleep.'

She kissed the phone, her scent strong on it again.

'Johnny? There's just one thing I wanted to ask you about this afternoon.'

'Yes, sweetheart?'

'You know the mole you had at the bottom of your spine.'

'Yes. What about it?'

'What happened to it? It wasn't there this afternoon.'

'I don't know what you mean. I can feel it now.'

'But—'

'Don't worry about it. Bury me in your pussy and keep me there until you come. Good night, sweet pussy. Sleep well.'

As the phone went dead, Ferne eased it sideways into herself. It was good that the handset was a smooth, slim modern one. She lay there watching the curved black thing plunging into her as she thought about the call. How did he get to Scotland so quickly after leaving her at Mai Lin's? Then, as she rubbed the handset between her labia and down over her bottom, everything dropped into place with a sickening crash.

He had been too young and too slim, his phallus too long and slender. Although he had said little, his voice had been much lighter and not so resonantly Scottish as she had remembered it. And there had been no mole at the bottom of his spine. She clenched her fists, kicked her legs repeatedly, put her head back and screamed with frustration.

'The dirty rotten, low-down, cheating bastard! He wasn't even there. He fobbed me off with someone else this afternoon.'

Chapter Five

LOOK, ROBERT, I thought I had made myself clear yesterday when I said that I wasn't prepared to consider any additional funding for Van Hagen Enterprises until we'd got control of the company.' Ferne glared up at the old man as he stood before her desk. She was not in a good mood anyway, and now this was making her more annoyed.

'You also said you couldn't attend the meeting with Van Hagen, Miss Ferne, and that it was about time some of us made a few decisions without you. We are very capable, you know. Some of us were running Daville with your father when you were . . .'

Ferne pre-empted the lecture with a raised hand. 'Yes – yes. I know all that, Robert. But I thought that . . .'

Now he put up his hand to stop her. 'You didn't hear the argument that young Van Hagen put up. The Board decided that we might lose our existing investment altogether if we didn't fund the last phase of the development.'

Ferne sat back and slitted her eyes. 'How much, Robert? How much did you agree to?'

'Half a million.'

She put her head in her hands. 'Christ almighty, Bob. That's crazy. That makes three and a half million we've sunk into that one company, and without anything to show for it so far.'

Now he shook his head slowly, keeping his eyes firmly on her face, holding his ground. 'But it was your decision to back old Van Hagen, Ferne. You did the figures. You said that when the material comes on to the market we'll make that much a year from licences alone.'

Ferne sighed and sat back. She felt drained. Suddenly her life was getting out of hand and she didn't like it. She had followed her own needs for a change and left the ship to the crew. Now when she got back on board they had gone off in a new direction. It was not her direction.

'I don't like it, Bob. And I don't want to do business with his son.'

Robert sat on the edge of her desk and studied her carefully. 'It's not like you to bring personal issues into our business dealings, Ferne. What happened between you and young Van Hagen?

She swivelled her chair away from him so that he could not see her face, and so that she could control her upset before turning back again. Across the city, the dome of St Paul's protruded through the heat haze of the summer morning. She swivelled back with determination.

'I don't want to talk about it, Bob.'

'You'll have to meet him sometime, Ferne. His father's too sick these days to run the show himself. He's made Jan Chief Executive. Jan's a bright fellow. You of all people should know that.'

She snapped up straight. 'No, Bob. I said no before and I'm saying it again. I don't want anything to do with ...' Her voice cracked and she swallowed hard to clear it. 'I don't want anything to do with Jan Van Hagen. Do I make myself clear?'

The old man stood up now, clearly on his mettle. 'I'm sorry, Miss Ferne. But as head of Daville, you'll have to meet him sometime. You can't let personal things get in the way of the Group's interests. Jan Van Hagen is back here to stay. He said that he called you a couple of months ago and told you so.'

He had called her three times, much to her annoyance. And he had sent her roses. She had steadfastly refused to see him. But this business of the additional capital was forcing her hand. She took a deep breath of resignation.

'Very well. Get him in, Robert. Today.'

'I'll try. But he might not be able to ...'

Ferne softened at the pleading look in the old man's eyes. She knew that she drove her people too hard and expected too much of them. But since she had started to develop her finer feelings, she didn't have the heart to wield the big stick as usual.

'All right. Do your best, Bob. And I'm sorry if I sounded off at you. I'm just a bit tense at the moment.'

He smiled an avuncular smile and nodded. 'You've worked too hard for too long, young woman. Finishing school then university, and then straight into the Chairman's role. I think it's time you began to live a little.'

She was just about to ask him what the hell he meant by that when she realised he had already left her office.

The next few days were hell.

Johnny did not call, and Van Hagen did not show. Robert Trenchard had made an appointment for a meeting which was now only ten minutes away. He had smiled as he had told her in a bad American drawl that Van Hagen had *'a very busy calendar'*. Jan Van Hagen had acquired a strong American accent since he had spent some years in the States. As Ferne recalled his former mellow Standard English, she shivered. But perhaps it was the words which she recalled which made the shiver, not just the memory of the voice. *Remember, Ferne, whatever happens, I'll always love you.*

This waiting to get the meeting with Van Hagen over with had made Ferne annoyed. Now she tapped her fingers on her desk, looking at the clock as the long hand reached the appointed time. Why was she so on edge? The past was past, and this was the kind of meeting she ran many times a day without a qualm.

As the clock struck twelve, her intercom buzzed. 'Mr Jan Van Hagen is here to see you, Miss Daville.'

Ferne was totally unprepared for the effect the tall, athletically built man had on her as he stepped into her office, his wide mouth smiling in an openly friendly way. His blue eyes lit with interest when they saw her. He had changed so much. Broader and more handsome than the youth of nineteen she had last seen, he looked every inch a man women would look twice at in the street. She had a difficult time stopping a blush creeping from her neck to her cheeks as she stood.

'It's very good of you to see me at such short notice, Ferne.' She detected a devilish glint in his eyes as he put out a long hand and took hers across her desk. 'It's been a long time, hasn't it?'

She took his hand firmly, shook it once and let go, a tingle shooting up her arm at the touch. He had tried to hold on for just a moment longer than she would have liked.

'You took your time coming in. Didn't my aide tell you that I wanted to see you urgently?' It was defensive and snappy, but why should she hide her annoyance with him?

An eyebrow raised slightly, but the face continued to smile, the blue eyes boring into hers. She dared not look away. That would signal her submission. So she held his gaze, coldly now and with a poker face as she sank into her chair, gesturing to him to sit as well.

He eased down slowly, leaning back in the chair. 'I'm sorry, Ferne, but I came as quickly as my schedule would allow.' The voice was rich and far more resonant than she recalled. It immediately reminded her of Johnny's voice even though her lover's intonation was Scottish Highlands.

'Well, now that you are here, I want to know just what this request for extra funding is all about. And if you don't convince me, I won't sanction it. Is that clear?'

'But your vice-presidents have already given us the green light, Ferne.'

'My "vice presidents" still need my sanction before the loan can go ahead, Mr Van Hagen.'

The smile left his face and his eyes went cold as he put up a palm towards her. 'I understand. But why don't we get to know each other again before we discuss such serious things?'

Ferne was floored. 'Look, Mr Van Hagen . . .'

'Jan – please, Ferne. What ever happened to us?'

She tossed back her hair. 'There was no "us" after you went off to America and got married. And I'm not in the habit of chattering about personal things in the office. I do brisk business here. Straight to the point and no holds barred. I find that's the best way, don't you?'

He smiled. 'If that's how you really want it. Absolutely no holds barred.'

'Good. Now if you'll just present your plan, I'll . . .'

He leaned across the desk, disconcertingly close to her. 'My plan, Miss Daville, is to get to know you again. Afterwards, I consider we would better understand what each of us wants from the relationship and that would enable us to accommodate each other's needs without future argument. Don't you think so?'

Ferne rose. 'Now look. If you think you can come . . .'

'Sit down, Ferne. You might scare your board of old men but you don't scare me. You never did.'

Ferne sat, the blue eyes across from her seeming to divine her soul. Her stomach was heaving, her heart thumping. Her breasts were tightening and her clitoris was beginning to transmit those feelings which had played such an annoyingly prominent part in her life over the past few days. Damn. This was crazy. Before Johnny had stripped her naked and taken her to bed, she'd had none of this kind of problem with men. And she had thought that she had banished Jan Van Hagen from her emotions years ago.

'It is not my intention to scare anybody. I just . . .'

The smile returned to the blue eyes as he sat up straight. 'Good. Then may I start by inviting you to lunch?'

Ferne breathed deeply, trying to get herself under control. Her enforced lack of sexual fulfilment and Johnny's deceitful conduct had played havoc with her emotions. She had even eyed up the office boy, imagining stripping him as he stood shyly in front of her.

'I'm sorry but I can't . . .'

'Can't or won't, Ferne? Are you still as stubborn as you always were?'

'I can't have lunch with you. I have a long-standing engagement.'

'I did not think you were engaged to be married?'

There was a slight but unmistakable mocking note in the riposte.

'I'm not engaged in that way, and I doubt that I ever shall be. Anyway, how did you know that?'

He smiled and locked his eyes on hers once more, strumming a leather briefcase with his long fingers. 'I've researched your career well, Ferne. I believe in knowing my allies and my opponents better even than they might know themselves.'

She leaned back in her chair, trying desperately to put on the air of nonchalant control she usually employed so successfully. 'This is a business meeting, Mr Van Hagen. I'm not applying for a job in your company.'

'Quite so. But if we are going to consider a marriage, I need to know every little mound and hollow of the person I will marry.'

'I beg your . . .' She sat bolt upright again.

'Don't beg, Ferne. It does not become you. I meant a marriage of our companies. I believe that you want an equal say in our affairs?'

'I want control. Nothing less.'

He shook his head. 'A good marriage works on a fifty-fifty basis, Ferne. It needs a bit of give and take.'

The deep American cadences took the tone of lecture out of the remark, but it made her bristle all the same.

'And what exactly do you propose to give?'

'Half the profits in Hagenite.'

'And what do you intend to take?'

'Another half-million sterling to take us to production.'

'Is that all?' She threw her head back with annoyance, a slight sneer purposely colouring her words.

He shook his head. 'Not quite.'

She raised an eyebrow, holding his eyes, more in control now as this was business talk. But Van Hagen kept her waiting for too many seconds for her liking, so she prompted him.

'What else do you want, Van Hagen?'

He produced the smile again. 'I want to make love with you, Miss Daville.'

Two more unhappy days passed before Johnny called.

Ferne had given Van Hagen short shrift and seen him out of her office, telling him that he could whistle for the money. In turn he had told her coolly that without the money the whole project might be lost, and her investment with it. Also, as for making love with him was concerned, she would have to wait now until he was ready for her.

The phone by her bed rang at eleven-thirty.

'Cleo?'

She nearly slammed it down. Then she recalled another investment that she would lose if she didn't follow through. 'I don't want to talk to you, Johnny.'

'Why not, sweetheart?'

'Because you deceived me. You made me think I was making love to you. I didn't know that man from Adam.'

He chuckled. 'You didn't know me either,

pussycat, but you still let me make love to you at Fanni's.'

She knew it was true and it annoyed her. But the confrontation with Van Hagen had stirred her up more. As far as men were concerned, she was in a greater turmoil than she would have imagined possible. She had been irrationally attracted to Van Hagen again despite his manner and assertions.

'Look, Johnny – I don't really care any more. I just need to get rid of this interminable ache you've started in me.'

'Come to the London house at two tomorrow.'

'I can't. I'm too busy.'

'Two o'clock or nothing.'

'But . . .'

'No buts, Cleo. If you want the next lesson, be there.'

The phone went dead.

Ferne was shaking as she pressed the bell-push at exactly two o'clock. Mai Lin gave her a friendly welcome. As she watched the ruby lips, Ferne's own lips recalled the full kiss she had received on her parting with Mai Lin. She had never kissed a woman on the lips before and it had proved to be strangely exciting.

Dressed in a flowing gown of silk, azure dragons breathing a fire of ruby stones as they wound around her slender body, Mai Lin looked radiant. Ferne felt that it was nice to see a friendly face which was not scheming something behind the smiling eyes.

'Is Johnny here, Mai Lin?' she asked as the young woman led her through to a bedroom.

'Sit down, Miss Cleopatra.' Mai Lin sat on the bed and beckoned Ferne to sit beside her. Ferne went to ask again, but Mai Lin held up a hand. 'The lesson today is to know yourself, Cleopatra dear. Tell me about the anger that you hold.'

Ferne was taken aback. Was this to be some kind of headshrinking session? Coldly she stood and looked down on the beautiful Asian woman.

Mai Lin smiled her winning smile and took her hands. 'Do not be cross. I want to share so much with you.'

Ferne sat, her hands still held by the slender fingers.

'Tell me why you are angry inside.'

Ferne shook her head. 'I don't know. I think I must have been born like it. Sometimes I really hate myself for it.'

'But within you I see a sensual creature with so much to give. Why do you hold it back so jealously?'

Ferne's eyes watered. 'I try to let it go. I did let go with Johnny for a while. And with that other man who was here last time I came.'

'That was Mark. He is really very beautiful; do you not think so?'

Ferne nodded her head. This was not entirely what she had expected from the afternoon, but it was pleasant to share things with another woman.

Mai Lin gripped Ferne's hand tightly. 'Mark is a wonderful lover. Do you like to make love, Cleopatra?'

Ferne nodded again. 'I like it more than I ever thought possible. But it scares me. Since I made love with Johnny, I've lost control of my life. Everything seems to be going wrong.'

Mai Lin smiled and stroked a lock of hair away from Ferne's forehead. 'Is that not because you try to make others do what you wish all the time?'

Ferne nodded again. Yes she did. But she had been brought up to it and had never questioned it until now. She had been surrounded by people who did exactly as they were told. She had been schooled to run the business since fifteen years of age, and at twenty-five had more experience in it than many men of forty. But she found it difficult to let go, of the business and of herself.

'I find it very hard to relax, Mai Lin.'

'Then you must let go of some things. You must allow yourself to be taken along with the wind at times. Only then will you smell its sweet scents and be lifted by its warm and loving currents.'

'But there's so much at stake. I can't afford to let go too much.'

'You must allow others to make their mistakes and you to make your own. Be honest with yourself. Tell yourself what you really want in life and be true to that.'

Ferne studied the slanting eyes, as clear as crystal backed with polished jet. They seemed to emanate wisdom, strangely moving in one so young.

Mai Lin took Ferne's hands again. 'Now we will learn how to give and to receive love. There will be no pressure as with men. There will be no hurry. We will take as long as we need to take.'

Ferne's eyes opened wide. Was she hearing correctly? Was she expected to make love with Mai Lin? Her heart skipped excitedly at the thought.

Mai Lin smiled. 'Let go, Cleopatra. Just allow yourself to love and to be loved without conditions. Expect nothing. Give what you wish to give. Then gradually learn how to give everything, and receive all in return.'

'But I gave everything to Mark. I got nothing in return except frustration.'

'Did you not get enjoyment from giving Mark joy?'

Ferne nodded. She had. She had received enormous enjoyment from her exploration of Mark's nakedness. And she had orgasmed as he had gushed his fluid over her.

'You're right. But I was just hoping for more. Something for myself.'

'Then you will get it in good time. But now learn to relax and to love and to be loved without any expectations.'

To Ferne's surprise, Mai Lin rose and stood before her as she sat on the bottom of the large bed. Mai Lin released her gown and slipped it off, revealing the most perfectly formed female body Ferne had been close to. Her breasts were completely rounded, slung in a lacy, half-cup bra. A diaphanous white triangle covered her pubis, two fine laces arching up over prominent hip bones, tied behind her waist. Her honey-brown skin was silky and undulating, a deep oval navel set in the softly-rounded cushion of her stomach.

The white triangle pointing downwards drew Ferne's gaze to a pair of legs so graceful that she was sure that the young woman was a dancer of some skill. She pirouetted gracefully in front of Ferne as if to demonstrate the fact.

'Undress me, Cleopatra.' Now the honey-brown back was turned towards her, the waist falling inwards and flowing out again over a small, firm little bottom, the G-string fastened in a bow in the centre. The bra clasp was within touching distance. At first Ferne dared not touch. But, as Mai Lin stood in front of her, unmoving and undemanding, she felt obliged to undo the bra.

The mirrors around the room showed reflected views of many pairs of perfect breasts. Ferne had an impulse to put her hands around Mai Lin and embrace them, but she curbed it.

Now the G-string took her attention. A third string curved up between Mai Lin's legs, hiding between the deep cushions of her bottom until it emerged to join in the bow.

Ferne's hands shook just as much as they had when they had slipped Mark's zip to reveal his stiffening shaft. Almost reverently she pulled at the bow and allowed the white material to float to the ground. Mai Lin opened her legs as she bent to pick it up.

The pair of softly formed sex-lips at the level of Ferne's eyes made her draw a breath. It was the first time she had viewed a woman between the legs.

As Mai Lin stretched and straightened, Ferne was faced with her nakedness, not knowing quite what she should do. She wanted to run her hands over the peach-soft bottom, to turn Mai Lin around and admire what the mirrors were seeing.

Feeling more secure now in the aura of permission which Mai Lin had instilled in the room, Ferne stood. Close but not touching, she set her mouth to the slender neck. The skin was warm, silky to touch, and alive with a vibrant energy. A tremor rippled through the lovely body.

'Thank you. That was very nice. Would you like to touch me more?'

It was so simply said, and the words embodied the sanction Ferne considered she needed to be able to touch Mai Lin's body. It was all so different from touching herself. It was so loving and permissive. Ferne felt no abhorrence, no guilt and no sense of dishonour to her sex. Why should one woman not love and admire another? Why should all loving come from men and go to men?

Ferne laid her hands lightly on Mai Lin's shoulders.

Mai Lin turned. Her eyes were bright, her mouth curved in a brilliant smile. And as she reached up to take Ferne's face between her hands, the perfectly formed breasts hung fully, the nipples dark and proud.

Ferne's breasts responded to the closeness of Mai Lin's, her own nipples stiffening quickly. Her stomach tightened and her secret lips felt warmly engorged. That urgent ache she had arrived with stayed quiescent.

'You are very beautiful, Cleopatra. Far more beautiful than I.'

Ferne shook her head. 'I think you're the most attractive woman I've ever seen. I wish I could be so calm and so accepting as you.'

'You can be whatever you wish to be, Cleopatra. Believe me.'

As Mai Lin held Ferne's face, her own face floated closer, the highly bowed top lip glistening invitingly. And when their lips touched it was like two butterflies alighting, savouring the nectar of a flower and departing again with hardly a flutter.

Ferne closed her eyes, unable to control the tremor in her stomach, her breath pulling heat into her chest as if Mai Lin were a fire radiating its brightly glowing warmth to her.

Now the oriental hands left her cheeks, took her tee shirt by the hem and slipped it over her head. Prepared for Johnny to strip her, Ferne wore no bra. She stood exposed to the searching eyes, watching their gaze slip admiringly over her breasts, taking in her smaller, pinker nipples, and her pale, taut stomach.

Mai Lin's hands returned to Ferne's face, slipped to her neck and traced the upper curves of her breasts until the tips of her forefingers alighted on the nipples. These stood proudly to attention, wanting to reach out and touch the long, brown nipples only a few inches away.

As if reading her mind, Mai Lin dropped her

hands to Ferne's waist, and swayed towards her. When their nipples touched, they were a perfect match, the tips of each contacting so lightly that Ferne could hardly feel Mai Lin's. Now her mouth met Ferne's again, and they stood, mouth to mouth, nipple to nipple, all Ferne's attention centred on the two firm points of the oriental breasts.

Gradually, Mai Lin leaned closer until both sets of breasts nestled cosily. Together they hugged each other, saying nothing, their breathing in unison, their breasts caressing warmly. Ferne closed her eyes and floated. How long the embrace lasted, she did not know, but, as Mai Lin pulled away, she felt a sadness, like an infant deserted in its cot at night.

Now Mai Lin knelt before Ferne. She undid the belt of her jeans and slipped the zip. Ferne had worn only a very skimpy pair of panties. She allowed Mai Lin to strip her slowly.

Mai Lin placed her lips against the lacy panties and held there for a moment before sliding them away. Her breath felt hot on Ferne's pubis, rippling underneath her. She widened her stance to feel the heated breath better on her labia.

Now Mai Lin raised herself, kissing up Ferne's stomach to her breasts, taking each in her lips for a few seconds before reaching Ferne's mouth. Taking Ferne's hands, she guided her to the bed so that they lay on their sides facing one another.

Ferne's fingers traced Mai Lin's breasts, toying with the nipples before moving to her lips. She traced the fine mouth with a finger tip, gliding it over the curves of the top lip formed like an archer's bow. And when she had done that, she slid down the bed and took Mai Lin's nipple in her mouth.

Mai Lin embraced her as she suckled the teat, firm between Ferne's lips. And as Mai Lin held her, Ferne wept, tears of joy and sadness.

Ferne sobbed, and as she sobbed, her body began to relax. It seemed to be shedding a tension which had held in her anger all her remembered life. For the first time she recalled her mother; very briefly. Then she was gone.

Now Ferne moved upwards, took Mai Lin's mouth and held there, needing to be rocked and kissed.

Mai Lin kissed her unreservedly and pushed her leg between Ferne's so that the softness of her sex kissed Ferne's thigh and Ferne's kissed hers. Their stomachs and their breasts heaved gently against each other, while their now warmly lubricated secret lips began to ride.

Ferne's breasts and her labia became engorged. As the gentle riding of one against the other quickened, the undemanding kiss blended into passion. The hand against Ferne's bottom began to claw. The fingers began to slide through the deep groove between her buttocks and to press into the little secret hole they found there.

Ferne's breath quickened, her hips flexed and heaved as the sensations on her mouth and sex and anus built steadily.

Mai Lin moved. She released her caress and turned, kissing Ferne's stomach as she went, until she had her head between Ferne's legs. She bent her own leg upwards, the sole of her foot on the bed so that Ferne could place her mouth against Mai Lin's secret lips. Ferne responded, bending her leg too so that she could feel her lover fully as Mai Lin kissed her.

Now Ferne studied the form before her eyes. Mai Lin had no body hair at all. The prominent triangle of her pubis led Ferne's gaze down between two softly formed labia, engorged but turned inwards, making a deep groove as an entrance for a man. Between these in-turned lips, a large clitoral nub nosed out, inviting her to kiss it. She took it and sucked, her tongue teasing gently, thrilling to every little tense movement Mai Lin made. And as she suckled, Ferne breathed deeply of her lover's scent, an erotically stimulating blend of musk and sweetness.

Ferne's own nubbin was throbbing now to the reciprocal attention it was getting. This was so different from the manner in which Johnny had taken her in his mouth. That had been so exhilarating, but this was breathtaking in its simplicity. She did not feel the same way about this as she had done when Johnny had prepared her to accept him.

The mutual suckling became more passionate as hands kneaded breasts and fingers plucked at nipples, legs widening, hips thrusting on to tongues.

Ferne flooded warmly. The whole of her body fired to a pleasant heat as energy washed up and over her, setting her cheeks aglow, her breasts pulsing.

Mai Lin groaned in her ecstasy, her legs opening and closing rhythmically as Ferne eased her through her climax, using all her natural sense as a lover.

Afterwards, in each other's arms, Ferne looked up at the mirrors above, seeing a pair of nymphs, one pinky-white against the honey-coloured tone of her lover, their faces alight with pleasure.

They dozed.

When Ferne woke, she was on her side, looking up at Mai Lin. Stretched out leanly along Ferne's length, and supported on one elbow, the other woman studied Ferne.

Between them was a tray of exotic foods, all arranged in delicate Chinese porcelain bowls so thin that they shone translucently. There were finely embroidered napkins, and little bowls of green tea sent a herby curl of vapour to Ferne's nostrils.

She smiled at Mai Lin. 'I feel marvellous. I feel so free for the first time I can remember. That nagging tension seems to have melted.' She stretched out to touch Mai Lin's hand. 'Thank you. How can I ever repay you?'

'You have already paid me with your love. Now eat. I am sure you must be hungry.'

Ferne munched at little pieces of carrot and celery and nuts and apricot. She sipped at the green tea and sucked on fresh lychees. They chattered as if they had known each other for years. It certainly seemed that way.

'Mai Lin?'

'Yes, Cleopatra.'

'Do you have other woman lovers?'

She nodded and touched Ferne's hand.

'Sometimes. But you are special.'

Ferne felt a rush of pride. It had made her feel special.

'Can we do this again one day?'

'Perhaps. But this kind of loving is no substitute for a man, Cleopatra. Being loved by a man, being taken forcibly and fucked, has a different range of sensations. I am addicted to it. And you?'

'I think I'm beginning to be. But – but what we had was different.'

Mai Lin smiled.

'But still it does not replace that sense of power we can have over a man as we take him into ourselves. Nor that explosion of fire raging through us as he takes us with such urgency it sucks away our breath.'

Ferne knew that she was right. But their loving had seemed so unthreatening.

'Do you have many lovers, Mai Lin?'

'Yes, I have many lovers, Cleopatra. It is my living.'

Ferne was taken aback a little. Then she rationalised her feelings. She was here for the same purpose men came for. What was the difference?

Ferne took a deep breath. 'Mai Lin?' She suddenly felt serious. 'Tell me about Johnny.'

Mai Lin's eyes studied her closely as if she were weighing something up. 'Johnny is a wonderful man, Cleopatra. I met him in America. I love him very much.'

Ferne felt herself go cold. She swallowed and tried not to let it show. Mai Lin touched her hand.

'But I am not in love with him. He comes to me when he needs to. Sometimes we just sit and talk while he tells me all his problems. Sometimes he just walks in, strips me roughly and fucks me hard and leaves with hardly a word. At other times he makes long and tender love to me. Sometimes I tease him and refuse him, fighting him like a she-cat. Johnny loves a battle with a woman. It makes him at his best. He is clever and witty and very, very sexy. You were fortunate to have Johnny as your first lover.'

'Don't you sometimes get fed up with the way they treat you?'

Mai Lin smiled and shook her head.

'I never get fed up, Cleopatra. I need to be loved and to be taken, constantly. It is in my nature and I do not fight it. I use it to my advantage.' She waved a hand gracefully at the opulent room. 'But do not fall into a rut, my love. I do not see my men if it does not suit me. Sometimes when they demand, I refuse. It makes them take me more passionately when I let them come.' She smiled demurely but her eyes lit up. 'Men need sex in different ways too. If you are going to be a good lover, there will be times when you should be willing to give yourself unreservedly. This is exhilarating in itself. Then at other times you may love and be loved. Fucking and loving are two different things. With fucking he simply wants to fill this with his cock – she slipped her hand between Ferne's legs and ran it through her labia – and to gush urgently inside you. With loving, he wants to experience every inch of your body and every long stroke he makes inside you. Both fucking and loving can give equal pleasure. If you demand one at the exclusion of the other, you might get neither.'

'You're very wise, Mai Lin.'

She smiled. 'I am very experienced with men. And as you gain in experience you will become wise with them too. I will teach you.'

Ferne and Mai Lin showered together, each soaping and massaging the other sensuously. They giggled like adolescents, and when Mai Lin splashed Ferne with cold water and ran into the bedroom, Ferne chased her and threw a pillow at her. It burst in a snowstorm of feathers, sticking to their damp skins. They rolled and tickled and laughed. And then they kissed.

The tension built so explosively, Ferne lost her breath. She threw back her head and moaned as Mai Lin bit her throat, sucked on her breasts and slid downwards. Then as she took Ferne between the legs, Ferne opened widely, straining herself to give her lover access. And as Mai Lin ate at her in a frenzy of passion, she screamed with ecstasy and sobbed, her body wracking with the sensation, her hips raised from the bed.

They dressed each other, wiping away the feathers, each laughing, each acutely conscious that they must part. Then, at the door, Mai Lin kissed Ferne long and tenderly, holding her hands, closing her eyes as she did so to hide the little tears which Ferne saw forming in the tear-drop eyes.

'Goodbye until next time, Cleopatra.'

Ferne snapped her arms around Mai Lin and held her tight. 'Oh my God, Mai Lin. I think I've fallen in love with you.'

Mai Lin smiled. 'For a little while, perhaps. But soon you will meet a man and you will manage him far more wisely than when we first met.'

Chapter Six

'MORNING, ROBERT.' FERNE breezed into her office, passing the old man in the corridor with a wave. He followed her in.

'Good morning, Miss Ferne. You look like a cat with three tails.'

She smiled. 'Sit down, Bob. I want to talk to you.'

'And I want to talk to you, Ferne. We've got to settle this matter with Van Hagen.'

'I thought I'd settled that. I told you what impudence the man had.'

He raised his hand. 'I know what you told me. But business is business and the Board agreed to advance the loan.'

Ferne scowled at him playfully. 'Have you bought any more of Van Hagen's stock yet?'

'We've got a few shares, but they're proving hard to get hold of. Some of the shareholders want a premium.'

'Pay it, Bob. I want control. Even if you have agreed the loan, I want more security. And I want Mr Van Hagen just where I can control him too. I'll teach him that he can't play fast and loose with me and get away with it unscathed. I'll control him in a way that he won't like.'

Robert gave her a look of desperation.

She grinned. 'Now I want to talk to you about something more important.'

He slitted his eyes. Clearly he did not trust her mood.

'I want everyone to have a bonus for their holidays, Bob. Ten per cent of their salaries.'

Trenchard was clearly lost for words. He studied Ferne closely. 'But we don't have the budget for . . .'

She raised her hand to stop him. 'Have Accounts work out the amount. I'll move it across from my personal account. I want it to be my treat.'

As the days flew past, faces at the office seemed much brighter, the whole atmosphere lighter. Ferne endorsed the funding for Van Hagen and kept her pressure on Robert to acquire the shares she needed for control. But someone else was in the market, competing for the stock. Ferne needed six per cent more to gain outright control.

The weekend loomed. It was the time of the annual meeting of heads of all the Daville businesses, together with their spouses.

Her father had always thrown open the big house at Capthorne Beeches for the weekend and she had kept up the tradition. This year she had been looking forward to it less than ever, but now her feelings had changed, she was determined to make it pleasant, if not fun.

Driving down to the house from the oppressive atmosphere of London in the summer heat, she had the top of the Rolls down. The stereo played Richard Clayderman. The wind tugged at her hair. She felt really free.

Nearing the house, the lanes grew narrow, over-reached by avenues of beeches and oaks. Sunlight dappled the road ahead with splashes of fawns and gold, and the canopy shone with myriad greens. In short, Ferne was happy. Johnny had not phoned since her session with Mai Lin, but somehow she didn't need him so much.

A red sports car streaked past, pushing her to the side of the road, the horn blaring loudly. It had been weaving behind her for some time. She frowned. Then, when she turned in at the gates to the Beeches and found the red car parked across them, she frowned more deeply still.

'Hello, Ferne.' The radiant face of Jan Van Hagen smiled down on her as he bounded to her side, his eyes sparkling with mischief, the arm of a dark blue blazer resting nonchalantly on her door.

She kept cool as she gave him an icy stare. 'Why are you blocking my driveway? And what the blazes are you doing here anyway?'

He grinned. 'Is that the correct way to greet your weekend guest, Miss Daville?'

Ferne snorted. 'You can forget that. I invited your father and mother, not you.'

He shook his head at her. 'Poor old Pops couldn't make it. And Mumsy wouldn't dare leave him. So, Ferne my love, I'm afraid you're stuck with me for the whole of the weekend.'

She scowled and then glared up at him, his mouth disconcertingly close to hers. 'Very well, if we're burdened with you for the weekend, I suppose we'll have to suffer it, but the invitation states quite clearly that guests are not expected until tomorrow afternoon.' She pointed a disparaging finger at the low red car. 'So I'll ask you to move that thing and let me get on.'

He raised an eyebrow at her. 'That "thing", Miss Daville, happens to be a very expensive Ferrari, and it cost at least as much as this old bucket of yours.' He patted the powder-blue leatherwork of the Rolls deprecatingly, pretending by studying his finger tips that it was dusty.

Ferne tapped her fingers impatiently on the wheel. 'Then it's a pity you didn't sacrifice your car to finance your project.'

He smirked. 'Why are you so mad at me, Ferne? Is it because I'm buying up our stock so you can't get control of my father's corporation?'

She felt herself tense. 'I might have known it was you. Well, we'll see who gets control first, Van Hagen.'

'Want to take a bet on it?'

'I never bet.'

He grinned. 'Scared you'll lose? I already have two more stock holders willing to sell. That puts me within two per cent of gaining absolute control.'

'And we have our fingers on the shares we need,

Van Hagen.' It was a bluff but she was not going to be bested by him.

'Ten thousand sterling says that I win.' He leaned further towards her. 'Unless of course you can't raise that much cash personally.'

'You're insane.'

'I'll sell my car and pay you ten ithousand if you get the control you're after, Ferne. If not – you pay me.'

She looked at him coolly, his wide mouth taking all her attention off what she should be thinking. Then she shook herself out of the reverie. 'Very well. But you'll lose your money. Now – I thought I told you to go.'

He shrugged. 'Must I? As I'm here now, I wondered if it might be OK for me to stay the night with you. I don't want to have to drive all the way back to London and then come down again tomorrow.'

She slitted her eyes at him then smiled demurely. 'You thought wrong.'

He gave her an expression of mock hurt and put his hand on her arm. She tried to move away but had nowhere to go to without leaving her seat.

'I thought we might dine together and then have an early night.' He winked exaggeratedly.

'Then you're mistaken. And I'll trouble you to move that car.'

He folded his arms defiantly.

This was too much for Ferne. She swept out of the Rolls, keyed a number in on a pad at the pedestrian gate and slipped through before Van Hagen realised what was happening. He sprang forward, thrusting his leg through the gap to stop her slamming the gate. Too late, it crushed the leg between the ironwork and the frame. He let out a bellow and pulled it back.

As the gate lock clicked behind her, Ferne strode up the driveway, ignoring Van Hagen's angry shouts.

'Hello, Perkins. Is everything going to plan?' Ferne tapped her telephone impatiently.

'Yes, Miss Ferne. But I would like to go over the wine list and the seating arrangements for tomorrow's dinner. Could you come across to the big house?'

Ferne was just about to leave by the garden door to see the butler when the external phone rang. She took it on the kitchen extension.

'Yes.' It was a short, sharp yes, full of her exasperation.

'Hey, Cleopatra, what have I done to warrant such a reception?'

The line was very crackly as if from a car phone, but she recognised Johnny's voice immediately. 'Hello, Johnny. How are you?'

'I'm fine, lassie. I hear that you and Mai Lin got on well.'

Ferne smiled to herself. The sensations of her liaison with Mai Lin still lingered. If it hadn't been for Van Hagen she would still be in the good mood she had been for a couple of days.

'Thanks, Johnny. It was marvellous. I never

thought I would say that to you, but there it is. I learned so much from Mai Lin.'

'I'm glad, sweetheart. I hoped you would. You sound different, you know.'

'How different? Old and haggard?' She laughed freely.

'That different. You sound lighter and more carefree. I want to kiss you.'

'Then why do you keep ducking out on my lessons?'

'Sorry. I'm very tied up.' He laughed. She could imagine him being tied up and thrilled to it. Something in her wanted to tie up a man and take him at her own pace without any fear of retaliation. Mai Lin and she had talked about it for some time, and she had recommended Ferne to try it.

'Cleo? Cleo are you still there?'

'Yes I'm still here.'

'I want to make love to you, Cleo.'

'Are you sure you don't just want to tear my clothes off and take me like you do Mai Lin sometimes?'

A long whistle came over the line. 'Is that what you would like me to do with you?'

Ferne was in a whirl now. Yes it was. But she needed loving too. 'When can I see you, Johnny?'

'Next time at the London house.'

'Promise?'

'I promise.'

'When?'

'I don't know. Perhaps a week.'

'A week? Hell. I don't think I can last that long.'

'Sorry, sweetheart, but that's the best I can do. Haven't you got some nice young man you could practise with in the meantime?'

'That's disgusting.'

'Don't be a prude. I'm sure there must be someone who fancies you.'

'There's a creep who keeps pestering me.'

'Is he as ugly as hell, with two left legs and a dick as big as a gnat's?'

'Don't be vulgar. Actually he's quite raunchy, but he's a jerk.'

'Jerks can be good in bed too. Sometimes that's all they are good at.'

'Don't even mention it.' She wished she hadn't brought it up. Van Hagen was proving difficult to get out of her thoughts. If she didn't get back to Mai Lin's soon, she might cave in on her resolve to keep him at arm's length.

'Thanks for calling, Johnny. Ring me as soon as I can come up. And, Johnny?'

'Yes, sweetheart?'

'What's the lesson going to be?'

'Letting yourself go, and trusting your lover. Now, give me a kiss.'

She kissed the telephone tenderly as it went dead.

Ferne strode up the steps to Mai Lin's house. It had been a thoroughly disagreeable weekend, and she was fortunate not to have Van Hagen suing her for almost breaking his leg. He had gone round with a limp and a scowl all weekend and she had kept well clear of him.

Mai Lin's bright face snapped her out of her mood immediately she opened the door.

They hugged, and kissed lightly on the lips. Then Mai Lin led her down the hallway to a different door this time.

Ferne's heart thumped as Mai Lin took her hand, leading her gently into total darkness. Without the warm hand in hers, Ferne would have bolted.

The blackness was total. She did not need her mask.

The room had a warm, steamy feel to it, and there was a scent of incense which floated around Ferne's head and invaded her nostrils. She breathed deeply and whispered, 'What are we going to do, Mai Lin?'

Mai Lin took both her hands and kissed her cheek.

'The lesson today is to learn how to let go and trust.'

'But how is it going to be different from . . .?'

Mai Lin's sweet-scented finger touched her lips. 'We will see, my love.'

Ferne felt Mai Lin's hands slide her blouse off so that she stood naked to the waist. But this time she could not even see her breasts as they tightened to the delicate touch of Mai Lin's fingers on her nipples.

As her jeans fell away under the dextrous fingers, she stepped out of them obediently. Mai Lin's arms came around her waist. Their bodies kissed: breasts and stomachs, pubic mounds and thighs, as well as mouths. It felt so safe.

Mai Lin took Ferne's hands and guided her through the pitch-black room until a warmth and an intoxicating aroma surrounded her. It came from a bath. To Mai Lin's gentle guiding, Ferne entered, the water neither hot nor cold. She sensed it about her calf only by its movement, not by its temperature.

To Ferne's surprise, she floated, just like she had floated once in the Dead Sea, the body-temperature water almost intangible.

'Now, Cleopatra, just relax. I will not leave you.'

Sweet lips touched hers, held a moment and were gone.

'Mad Lin?'

'Yes, sweetest?'

'Johnny said he'd be here today. Is he coming?'

'Shhh. We will see.'

Ferne floated as if in space. There was no sensation: no sound. No touch. No light. Only the incense and her breathing told her that she was not a soul without a body, floating in eternity. Her awareness seemed to be all around her instead of in her body. It was not centred anywhere.

Then a breath of extra warmth fanned around her face. It was a different breath. A masculine scent, giving her a clean peppermint flavour as she took it into her mouth.

'Mark?'

Lips touched hers, strikingly warm in the void. She pursed her own lips to touch them. The kiss was tender, and as it floated away in the void, she felt deserted.

'Mark, is that you?'

'Hello, Cleopatra.' She smiled at the lightness in the voice. It evoked pictures of the slender body with its hardened penis curving up towards his navel.

'Yes, it's me.'

Ferne's heart beat a tattoo in her chest. She focussed on the space from which the voice whispered.

The lips took a nipple and held it. For Ferne, it was as if there was nothing else in the world but that small, throbbing nub. As she floated, all her attention was centred there now. There was nowhere else to focus it.

'Oh my God,' she moaned.

The mouth left the nipple and moved to the other. It stayed for some minutes, suckling gently, Mark's breath rippling the water which washed lightly over her stomach.

Then he left her to float alone again. For a minute she thought he had gone away, but breath on her mouth made her sigh with relief.

But this was different breath again. And the scent was the scent which had made her wild with passion on the first occasion she had smelled it. As the lips touched hers she breathed deeply.

'Johnny?'

'Hello, Cleo.'

Their lips embarked on an impassioned feast and when they stopped for breath, Ferne seemed to be floating at a higher level of sensation. She had not realised just how much she had craved to feel his lips again, to smell him and to have him near her. Van Hagen had come close. He too had mesmerised her. But he had challenged her in business and she would not back down an inch.

'Johnny?'

'Yes, Cleo.'

'Johnny are you going to . . .?'

'Am I going to what?'

'You know.'

He laughed. It was just a little expiration but she could imagine the wide, smiling mouth in front of her face.

'What do I know, Cleo?'

'You know what I want.'

He laughed again.

Now the whole of Ferne's world was centred in her clitoris. She floated in the bath of body-temperature water, her legs splayed, as a single finger contacted that part of her. It was as if no other part of her body existed.

Johnny worked gently, moving his finger slowly, tensioning the tissues of her labia as he drew the nubbin upwards, sliding down between them as he reversed his stroke.

'Ahhh. That's too nice.'

'Good. Shall I do some more?' The whisper came through the darkness like steam from the bath, hardly sensed but carrying a warmth which filled her. Warmth crept up from her clitoris too. It seemed to swell with pride at being the centre of his attention as well as hers. And as it engorged, the heat travelled into the area between her pubis and her navel. In the isolation from reality, she could feel the walls of her vagina, tensing and relaxing gently with every small stroke.

As the heat grew more intense, the contractions grew stronger, but not as strong as the orgasmic rigors which had wracked her the first time she had held Johnny inside her.

Now a new sensation was added to the central focus as two sets of lips each took a nipple. Gently they sucked, teasing and squeezing, and letting go, only to return again.

A triangle of warmth grew from Ferne's breasts downwards, while the heat from her nubbin continued its upward quest, until each met in the depths of her navel and fused.

The lips pulled now at the rampant nipples, making her body wave in the water, intensifying the sliding of the finger. As lines of fire flowed down towards the growing tension between her legs, she opened her mouth to pant. It sounded like a steam engine in the stillness: rasping and needful.

'Johnny?'

'Yes, Cleo?'

'Johnny – I don't want to come like this.'

'How do you want to come?'

His tone was more tender than before. On the last occasion he had phoned, he had sounded hard, as if something she had said or done had upset him. But that might have been due to the crackly line. Car phones often sounded harsh and indistinct.

'Johnny, I want your cock.'

'Then you shall have it, lassie, but don't forget the lesson. It's to learn to let go and to trust.'

'I trust you to fuck me nicely,' she giggled, the shamelessness coming from her growing need to orgasm.

At that, two strong pairs of arms cradled her under the hollow of her back. They raised her so that she hung in the air, her shoulders and head downwards, her legs drooping and her stomach arched.

She dripped, warmly.

And as she hung there totally trusting to the men's strength, a mouth came between her legs and suckled her while two others took her nipples. Her breasts were tight, compressed by the tension of her body and her nipples screamed their pleasure.

The tongue between her legs thrust aside her secret lips and pushed inside her sex. Ferne tensed and held her breath, opening her legs as widely as she could. They found Mai Lin's slender shoulders and wrapped around her neck to capture her.

Then they all moved, the mouths still locked to the nipples, the tongue working strongly between her pulsing labia and her clitoris. And when she was set down on the softness of a bed, it felt cold like plastic.

The darkness cloyed, but it seemed to contain little sparks of light as energy coursed through her.

She sighed.

The bed dipped as the weight of two people knelt beside her, another between her outstretched legs. Then a fluid heat crept over her navel and her breasts, carrying the warm scent of cloves, and the thick aroma of sandalwood.

Three sets of supple fingers set to work now; two plucking up her nipples then raising the weight of her breasts and letting go again.

The third pair of hands ran, flat-palmed, over her abdomen, circling and smoothing and spreading the heat of the aromatic oil over every millimetre of her skin.

Her shoulders, her neck and her face all received their attention, three pairs of loving fingers caressing fluidly. It was as if she were surrounded by attention. Then she let them turn her, relaxing her body totally, trusting them implicitly not to harm her in any way.

The sheet was slippery, filled with oil, the scent almost overpowering. It sent tingling energy down into the whole of her body. In contrast to the floating-bath, the oil drew attention to every part of her, sensitising her stomach and breasts, her inner thighs and arms.

They turned her and slid her downward so that she lay on her stomach, her knees on the floor, her breasts slippery with the lubrication. Then two powerful pairs of hands took her arms and worked the oil sensuously up and down them, culminating at her finger tips. They separated her fingers, massaged each one and then moved to her palms, making them come alive.

As the men's hands worked their magic, another pair of hands floated over her buttocks, diving down the deep valley of her bottom. The hands swept up and down, over her secret lips, pushed out by the kneeling position to gather more sensation from Mai Lin's touch.

Now two fingers entered her while the thumb massaged at her secret entrance, totally exposed as Ferne splayed herself for greater contact. The sensation of being touched there made her shudder with delight, the contact seeming to increase the pleasure in her clitoris and vaginal walls.

Then the men took her hands and guided them up their kneeling legs as they sat back on their heels. Each of Ferne's hands found a rigid phallus, straining with the excitation their masters had evoked in them. Her fingers closed on each stem, her thumbs finding the webs and massaging gently.

Each man let out a moan of pleasure.

But Ferne's concentration was drawn away from her pleasure-giving fingers, to the place between her buttocks which was receiving its own attention. Mai Lin's thumb was right inside her secret hole and two fingers inside her sex opened and closed her too, the sensation of both actions blending into one.

Ferne found herself opening to the fingers, eagerly receptive to their gentle probing.

Two strong pairs of arms now pulled her. She found herself sliding over the warm body of a man. He lay on his back so that as she slid upwards, his rock-hard organ ploughed between her breasts, across her stomach and over her pubis and came to rest between her legs.

Ferne's mouth explored the mouth which came to seek it, unsure with the aroma of the oil, which man it was.

'Hello, Cleo.' It was Johnny's voice and as its soft cadences reached her ears, she thrilled. She needed Johnny. For some reason he held a spell over her. Whether or not it was because she had given her virginity to him she did not know. Perhaps it was because he was leading her on such an erotic adventure that she was totally dependent on him as she had never depended upon anyone before.

'Hello, Johnny. My God, I love this so.'

They kissed passionately, his arms around her shoulders, her oily hair draped around his face.

'Love me, Johnny. Love me gently. I just need to feel your cock inside me. You can fuck me hard another time; but love me now.'

With a kiss on the nose and an expert change of angle, she felt his hardness slide into her. She was so slippery inside with the excitement and with the oil outside that he glided in with ease.

The slickness of the oil over their bodies enabled Ferne to work herself on him, drawing up so that he almost left her sex-lips, plunging down so that the root of his shaft rammed her clitoris. She began to pant, sliding more avidly over him, his mouth locked on to hers, her sex taking him in voraciously.

Then she felt another warmth on the back of her legs. Firm hands took her buttocks and kneaded, lending strong sensation to her labial contact with Johnny.

Ferne heard the tearing of foil and smelled the smell of rubber. She felt Mark kneeling, the insides of his legs against the outsides of her thighs. His hands worked up the hollow of her back, forcing her stomach tightly against Johnny's, her breasts against his chest. Then she felt a warmth on her secret place. It was hotter than Mai Lin's finger, and as it nosed into her, she felt it wider and stronger.

Ferne gasped at the sensation. The warmth of Mark's inner thighs over the back of her own thighs, and the heat of his phallus working into her secret little hole, made her force her bottom out. This made her engorged labia squeeze and thrust on Johnny all the more.

Mark slid into her with such gentleness that it was not painful. Ferne knew now that Mai Lin had prepared her well. As he pushed, she could feel the whole extent of him building up such a wonderful pain that she gasped again, her mouth devouring Johnny's mouth as he began to thrust into her other place.

'Oh my God,' she moaned as she panted and writhed, impaled by two men, trapped by Mark's weight, embraced in Johnny's arms.

'Ahhh, Johnny. Ahhh. Do it. Oh my God, don't stop now. Do it harder. Oh my God.'

Johnny thrust up into her. 'Feel me, Cleo.'

'And me, Cleopatra,' Mark laughed.

'I can feel you both like broom handles,' she gasped. 'But fuck me harder. I can't stand it if you don't.'

The climax came in a bolt of pure red energy which ripped through Ferne where both her lovers thrust deeply into her. Her body went rigid, trapping each shaft as they pumped.

She felt the surge of heat from Johnny as he flooded her, pumping with such power and urgency. She squeezed him hard between her legs, trying to prolong the sensation as much as she possibly could.

Working over Johnny made her bottom rise and fall and impale more sensuously on Mark's still-rigid shaft. In unison they pulsed and tensed and relaxed and pulsed again.

As they relaxed, Mark lay on top of Ferne, his weight supported on his elbows, his heat flooding her.

Suddenly Ferne had an impulse to turn herself under Mark, and pulled herself off Johnny's shaft to face up towards Mark. He eased back to let her complete the manoeuvre.

'Kiss me, Mark. And I want you in me, frontways. Please.'

As she lay with her back to Johnny's chest, his hands around her breasts, his tongue in her ear, Mark lowered his mouth to hers. Then as she felt him enter her, she groaned with pleasure.

She took him deeply into herself by wrapping her legs around his hips and held him there while he pushed gently in and out, his lips tenderly sucking at her mouth, his tongue imitating the action of his phallus.

After Mark had brought her to another orgasm,

he withdrew and thrust between her breasts, and she brought him to his climax, working his foreskin gently to milk him of every drop of semen that she could.

When he had ceased to pulse in her hand, they bathed her and laid her on a warm, dry bed of towels to pat her dry. Fingers between her legs, and in her secret place and under her arms, caressed and tantalised while she giggled.

After she had been powdered like a new-born baby, a pair of iron-strong arms lifted her to her feet. Lips kissed her all over, while others kissed her breasts and her inner thighs. And when the arms set her down on the bed again, Ferne felt so thoroughly sated with attention that she floated, her face smiling broadly, her eyes opened wide to the darkness.

'That was the most extraordinary experience of my whole life,' she whispered to the darkness.

Three sets of lips kissed her lips, one at a time, slowly and with great tenderness.

Then there was nothing.

'Johnny?'

No reply.

'Mark?'

Silence.

'Mai Lin?'

'I'm here, Cleopatra. I told you I would not leave you.'

'Where's Johnny, Mai Lin?'

'He's gone.'

'And Mark?'

'Yes. They both had to go. But Johnny will talk to you soon.'

'Thank them, Mai Lin. This afternoon has changed my life. I feel as if I've been reborn.'

Ferne felt alight as she entered the office in a fresh blouse and skirt but with no bra or panties. She wanted to feel open, the cool breeze between her legs. At her desk she thumbed absent-mindedly through papers. She had moved on with such strides in only a few weeks that the business of running the organisation seemed stultifying.

She wanted to fly; to be free; to live and to love and to catch up on all those things she had denied herself for years. Even through university she had kept herself apart. While others had revelled, Ferne had studied and calculated her days away.

Picking up a memo from Robert Trenchard, she toyed with it, musing upon how much she owed to him. She owed everyone such a lot.

Memo: Miss Ferne. From R.T. I have just heard that Van Hagen has secured a block of shares I was after. He paid well over the odds, my contact says. Sorry. Van Hagen now has forty-nine per cent of the holding. We have the other forty-nine. We both need two per cent more for outright control.

Screwing up the memo, she flung it in her waste-basket. Damn. And damn again. But Ferne was determined that this was not going to spoil her mood. Nothing – not even Van Hagen – was ever going to spoil that again.

The phone rang. Ferne was reluctant to answer.

She was off-duty. Before her emancipation she would have been working until ten or later. Now at seven o'clock she was finished. She was finished with all that hard work. She would still be efficient, conscientious and commanding, but not in the fanatical way she had been before.

The phone continued to ring and in exasperation she picked it up.

'Hello, Ferne. Are you speaking to me?' Van Hagen's voice was soft. It matched her mood but she slammed down the phone. It rang almost immediately, so she picked it up and hissed, 'Get off my line, Van Hagen. I don't have to talk to a jerk like you.'

'Do you want to talk to my attorney instead?' The voice was cold now. It made her shiver.

'What the hell would I want to do that for?'

'For inflicting grievous bodily harm on an innocent man. You nearly broke my leg in that damned gate of yours.'

Now her blood ran cold. Was he intending to sue her after all? Ferne sighed and shook her head. If she was going to leave Miss Iceberg behind for good, she should try it for everyone, not just the people she liked.

'I'm not going to discuss this on the phone, Mr Van Hagen.'

'Have dinner with me then.' It was a lightning-fast response and full of enthusiasm.

'Forget it. Come to my office tomorrow. My secretary will fit you in somewhere.'

'Oh no. I'm not having that kind of runaround

from you, Ferne Daville. If you want to avoid a lawsuit from me, you meet me face to face so you can apologise.' This time the voice held its usual fun.

'Me say sorry to you? You can forget—'

'No, Ferne. Say sorry nicely or I sue.'

Now she wasn't sure if he was serious or not. But that was no reason to let him get the upper hand. He was already within two per cent of retaining control of his company and she was in danger of losing the wager of ten thousand pounds if he got the shares.

Ferne put down the phone carefully and smiled. He could cool for a while at least.

An hour later, she was just about to leave when she saw a slip of paper under her door. Quickly she snatched it up, her fingers shaking as she opened it and read.

Dear Ferne, I love you. I have loved you from the moment we met when you were sixteen. I thought I knew you intimately before, but nothing prepared me for the bolt of lightning which ripped through me when we met recently. I'm devastated that I hurt you when I went to the States. If you have any feelings for me at all, please tell me how I can redress the balance.
Jan Van Hagen.

Ferne snatched open the door but the corridor was empty, only the caretaker rubbing at the brass-work by the lift.

'Did you see who put this note here, Mr Jenks?'

The man looked up somewhat shiftily she thought. 'No, Miss Ferne. There's been nobody past here this last five minutes.'

Silently she closed the door and put her back to it, tears streaming down her cheeks. Damn Van Hagen. And just as she was beginning to be happy too.

Chapter Seven

'JOHNNY, I THINK I'm going mad. I went to jelly when I read that note. I wanted to call him to come over and . . .'

'And what, Cleo?'

'And you know.'

'And let him take your knickers down and have his wicked way with you?' he chuckled.

'Don't laugh. I think I'm turning into a slut.'

'I warned you that once you found the libertine in you, you might find her difficult to control. But don't go making yourself wrong over this, Cleo. There must be something between you and Van Hagen to make you feel like that.'

'How do you know his name?'

'You told me.'

'Did I? I don't recall. Anyway, I don't want to talk about it. The man's a pig.'

'But you want him.'

'Sometimes I do. Then he makes my blood boil.'

'Why?'

'He's so sneaky. He must have slipped that note

under my door and then run away. He might at least have told me to my face how he felt.'

'Have you given him a chance to do that?'

'No – of course not.'

'Then perhaps it was the only way he could get his message across to you without you blowing up.'

'You sound as if you're on his side.'

'I can see his point of view, Cleo. You really are quite prickly when you get on your high horse.'

'I am not.'

'Yes you are. You're prickling now. The way I read it is that you're both attracted to one another. If the fellow has any brains, he knows you want him. Most men do know that. It's your feelings you've got to sort out. You can't go around fancying people and then blaming them for taking you up on it.'

'I've never been like this before.'

'Right. Haven't you been a closed-up, spoilt little iceberg who always got her own way? I think you're just learning what it's like to feel like a woman and to have to deal with other people's emotions as well as your own.'

'You sound like a head-shrinker.'

'I sound like someone who can see a butterfly emerging from its chrysalis but doesn't know that it's a butterfly yet. It's scared of stretching its wings and flying in case it crashes.'

'Oh God; you make me sound like a wimp.'

'A wimp wouldn't do what you're doing, Cleo. It takes great courage to do that. You've set out to learn all about your sexuality and you're doing all right. You'll settle down in a while.'

'But aren't you jealous?'

'Why should I be jealous? My job is to bring you out. The fact that you fancy that other guy means I'm doing my job well.'

'But I thought you and I . . .'

'No, Cleo. I've never promised you anything but to teach you about sex in all its forms. More than that wouldn't be fair to either of us.'

Tears blurred her eyes and she sniffed.

'Look, lassie, let's just see what happens over the next few weeks. Things might work out differently from what you expect.'

'But don't you love me, Johnny?'

'Of course I do, silly. You're beautiful, intelligent and capable. But that doesn't mean that you should expect me to marry you.'

'But . . .'

'No buts. Remember, I'm your tutor. My job is to help you learn – and fast.'

'I am learning fast.' She sighed deeply. 'When can I see you?'

'I'm going away for a while. I'll see you when I get back.'

'Will you ring me?'

'Of course. I want to know how you get on with the next lesson.'

'I don't know if I can . . .'

'Yes you can. And if you don't turn up – that's it. I'm only giving you one shot at this, Cleopatra. Flunk it and it's goodbye.'

'You're telling me that if I don't do what you want, you won't ever contact me again?'

'Right.'

'My God, Johnny, that's blackmail.'

'That's how it is, Cleo. You wanted to do this – so do it. The next lesson is at four on Friday.'

'But I can't just drop . . .'

'Four o'clock, sharp.'

She pouted to herself but she knew that there was no point in protesting further.

'What will the lesson be?'

'Learning to be submissive.'

'I can do without that.'

'From what you tell me, you seem to have to control everything. Perhaps it's time to feel what it's like not to be able to. Unless you know what that's like, you won't be able to switch it on or off. Learn how to give way a little, Cleo. Life for you seems to be one long battle. Now kiss me.'

She kissed the phone and put it down.

Mai Lin hugged Ferne as she entered.

Ferne was trembling. She had almost not come. Learning to be submissive seemed to her to be the hardest concept yet. Why should she submit to anyone or anything? She had always been a fighter. She had always got her way by knowing what she wanted and going for it. Nothing and no one had ever stopped her. Why should she change that now?

Anyway – she had been submissive to Johnny at

Fanni's. She had submitted to the two men in the oily bed. How would submitting to them again be any different?

Mai Lin led her along the corridor and stood waiting for her to catch up.

Ferne felt afraid.

'Do not fear, Cleopatra. Nothing will hurt you. Perhaps your pride will be a little bruised, but that will only be because you hold on to it so rigidly. If you can let it go and experience humility, you will learn much today.'

Mai Lin kissed Ferne's cheek and opened and closed the door for her. Ferne stood with her back to the door in a windowless room. It was sparsely furnished: a bed, a hospital couch, mirrors on the walls and ceiling, and some ropes hanging down from pulleys.

A movement caught her eye. To her left the naked figure of a very tall man stood by the wall. Black as ebony, his body appeared smooth, as if it were polished, his skin swollen with muscles shining in the light. He was already aroused. From a nest of wiry hair surrounding his pouch and matting his pubis, a phallus reared like a cobra, its single eye wide as if about to spit thick and potent venom.

Ferne shrank back as he flashed a set of teeth as widely as a half moon. Deep brown eyes shone as they scanned her figure from the vee in her trousers to her breasts hiding behind a pink summer blouse. She had worn pink to feel more feminine. Something in the subject of this lesson told her that she might need all her feminine wiles to keep herself safe.

Immediately the man stepped towards her, she knew that she would not be strong enough to overpower him, should she need to do so. Her heart drummed in her chest. Her temple beat in unison and her solar plexus tightened, trying desperately to still the thousand butterflies which struggled to get loose.

'Take your clothes off.' The voice boomed, resonating from a chest as wide and as polished as a double bass. A small whip which he smacked into one hand added menace to the command.

She shook her head. 'Oh no. I'm going to pass on this one, thanks very much.' She turned to leave, but the door was locked. There was no way out. Now she beat on the door with the flat of her hand.

'Mai Lin? Mai Lin, let me out.'

A rumbling laugh filled the room. Ferne spun to face the man.

'Don't you laugh at me. Just let me out or I'll . . .'

He laughed again, his hands on his hips, his phallus jerking to every ripple of the drum-tight stomach. 'Take all your clothes off, missie. Or I shall strip you myself.'

'Touch me and I'll . . .'

A bolt of lightning left his eyes and the moon-wide mouth flashed once again. 'If you don't undress, Miss Prim-and-Proper, I'll rip your clothes off. Do you want to go home in rags?'

Ferne shook her head. There was no way she was going to obey this man, handsome as he was in a brutal kind of way. Within two paces now, he towered over her, a skyscraper taller than herself. And, in proportion to his giant size, his penis was also huge. She had never imagined one could be that big. Closer now, it shone like a branch of burnished wood. The head glowed the purple colour of a Victoria plum, perched like a beret on the top of the brown-black pole. Veins pumped regularly around the girth of the pole, and as he strained it towards her, it swelled and stood out from his body.

She turned to the door again and screamed, her fists drumming wildly against solid oak. 'Mai Lin! I want to come out. Mai Lin! Please? I've changed my mind.'

Ferne felt her feet leave the ground. She hung in the air as a powerful arm clamped around her waist. Kicking did no good; her espadrilles flew in two directions.

He spun her around and almost threw her across the room so she landed beside the couch. Diving over it and behind it, without taking her eyes off his for a second, she felt the couch. It was like a maternity delivery table, padded and with separate arm, leg and head supports. She swallowed hard. There was no way he was going to have her on that. He'd squash her to a pulp.

He advanced.

She backed away, crouching like a cat, claws out, legs tensed ready to spring. At least she would do some damage before he overpowered her.

The whip, short, flat and flexible with some

small leather thongs at the end, thwacked in his palm again.

'Strip off everything. You'll do it eventually so why not now?'

'There's no way I'll strip off for you, you brute.'

He grinned, the teeth shining white as he thwacked the switch playfully. 'You will.'

'Never. I'm not submitting to you. No one ever gets the better of me.'

Ferne heard her voice saying the things she had always said in temper.

It was her stock retort to any problem which would not yield. That was what had made her so successful. But she realised now that it had brought her tension, and had attracted fear if not hatred from those she wielded power over.

'Strip.'

'No.'

'You will.'

'I will not.'

'We'll stay here until you do. All night. All day. All week?'

'You can't keep me here. I've got important business.'

He roared with laughter, his stomach panting deeply. 'So have I. You're my important business. I'm going to tame you before you leave, little cat. So why don't we start by being friendly?'

Ferne put her head on one side.

'How friendly?'

He worked his phallus in a long-fingered hand. 'This friendly.'

'You're not putting that thing near me.'

He nodded his head to refute her statement. 'And we will start by taking your clothes off. Then you will kiss my balls.'

'Go to hell.'

'And you'll tell me how you honour me. You will worship me with your eyes. They are the eyes of a tigress protecting her young. Oh yes, little missie, I see an angry creature hiding in you, and I'll loose it and tame it. You, tigress, will leave here with your tail between your pretty legs and you will know what it is to be humble.'

'Go to hell.'

He moved towards her, the mouth grinning wickedly now.

She skipped away.

They stalked around the couch.

He lunged, vaulting the couch with seemingly effortless ease.

She dived for the bed, rolled over it and sprang on her feet, the giant closing in on her. He had her cornered now.

Ferne kicked out.

That was fatal. He caught her foot and turned her, spinning her, laughing at her helplessness, her free leg and arms flailing vainly. Then to her horror she felt herself rising. He had her foot in some kind of sling and was winching her into the air. She kicked out with her free foot but he caught it deftly and trussed it too. Now she was hung like a ham, her legs splayed, her head down, her stomach opposite his chest.

'Let me down.' She struck him hard. He laughed and winched her higher. Now her crotch was at his shoulders. She wriggled and snaked and shook, but to no avail.

As if skinning a rabbit, he pulled her blouse apart, the buttons pinging around the room.

'You moron. Do you know how much that cost?' She tried to swing and butt him in the testicles, but he stepped nimbly out of her way.

Then she saw the knife. Oh God.

With no more ado than if he were gutting a herring, he slit her trousers, not even bothering to undo the belt. Cleanly he sliced up the legs so that they just dropped away.

'You cretin. Those were originals. You can bloody well pay for them.'

Ferne was acutely conscious that she was naked apart from her panties, her breasts lolling downwards, her stomach heaving with a mixture of fear and excitement. So far he had not hurt her. Mai Lin had promised that. But what if he suddenly lost control in a fit of lust?

Almost delicately he slipped the knife blade under the band of her panties. She watched the black hair of her mound emerge through the slit. Then the flimsy garment floated to the floor under her. Now he looked into her crotch, open to the smiling eyes. He only had to move slightly and his mouth could take her. She began to pant.

It was the touch of the switch across her labia which made her freeze. The leather thongs just touched her lightly but they stung exquisitely. Immediately Ferne felt herself swell. It was stimulating rather than painful and her body was responding to it.

He switched her again, and again, each touch setting her labia afire. She could feel her sexual mouth begin to open and shut in small orgasmic waves. The man was a devil. And all the time she was looking up at the great thing between his legs, towering above her. Something perverse in her wanted to lick his testicles. She told herself that she was a slut and she reprimanded herself harshly for it. Apart from that, there was no way she was going to give in to him.

Ferne shuddered as he ran a finger through her groove, wet now with the stimulation of the whip.

Again she wriggled but to no avail.

He knelt, his face close to hers.

'Now, little lady, are you going to be a good girl and do as you're told?'

'Go to hell.'

'Go to hell, master.'

'Go to hell, bastard.'

He moved around her so she couldn't see him. But she felt him. The switch landed on her buttocks. The second stroke came between them, just tipping the sensitive area around her little hole.

She gasped.

As he whipped again, her buttocks began to sting.

Now he knelt behind her, his hands running down her body, and over her breasts. The great hands were so large that he held each breast in one palm. Then the hands moved downwards, and before she knew what was happening, both wrists were tied together in a noose. A line was hooked on the noose. She was turned, the ropes on her legs slackening while the other raised her.

Now she was upright, strung up by her arms, her feet tied together too, her body under his control. But there was no way he was going to control her spirit.

The face came perilously near.

It was a strong face, angular as if sculpted from ebony and then rounded and polished. He was actually quite handsome, his eyes clear and shining with that sparkle of fun which took the menace out of his nearness.

A large, pink tongue licked broad lips which reminded her in thickness and in succulence of a woman's labia. But when they smiled, the fun which emanated from them warmed her.

'Now then, Cleopatra. Do you see how weak you are? Do you see how easy you are to control?'

'Shut up and get on with whatever it is your perverted mind has planned. I can see that I can do damned all about it. But you'll never break my spirit.'

He shook his head.

'That is not what we're here for, even though I might do what I like with you.' He bent and took each nipple in turn to prove the point. 'And I might treat you to this.' He bent his phallus outwards and forced it between her legs. Here he sawed it through her groove until her clitoris began to come to life. As he withdrew, the veined shaft twanged upright again, and she was almost disappointed. 'And I can whip you until you beg me to stop.' The tassels of the whip caught a nipple lightly and made her flinch. But the nipple stood to attention just the same. 'So you see how I can do whatever I want to with you. But what I want is for you to pay me homage. You will kneel before me and you will kiss my feet. And you will suck on my cock until I come in your mouth. And you will thank me, and beg me to take you. Do you get it?'

'Go to hell.'

'Go to hell, master.'

'Go to hell, prick.'

The switch stung across her breasts and made her twitch. She set her face in angry defiance. 'I said go to hell.'

Smiling wanly, he took her around the waist, unhooked her wrists and held her across his body. With her wrists tied and her feet trussed, Ferne was helpless in the giant's arms. He smelled of male, both musky and sweet at once, the aroma seeming to resonate in her nostrils, sending messages of lustfulness deep between her legs. But his breath was peppermint fresh as he lowered his lips to hers. Mesmerised, she watched them coming down, so succulent and inviting. She was surprised as her lips pursed to meet them. But they stopped smiling and withdrew. He was playing with her, pleased at her response.

She pouted.

As he set her on the table, she watched a mirror on the ceiling.

Now he inspected her, his face seeming to be admiring her, his eyes glinting but not – she judged – with lust.

The great hands caressed her all over, as light and as fleeting as feathers blown on a summer's breeze. She felt loved, not violated, by the touch.

Ferne did not struggle, knowing it would be in vain. There was something about the man which instilled awe in her.

Now he fastened a strap around her neck and the headrest so that she was captured. If she tried to raise her head, it choked her.

She stared up as the man towered over her and she viewed herself in the mirror above. Her breasts heaved as she breathed rapidly with a mixture of fear and excitement while he undid her wrists and fastened each separately to an arm rest with leather straps. Her arms were above her head, her palms facing upwards. This stretched her breasts and made them flatten to her chest. The nipples hardened although she willed them not to.

Now as she lay spread out, she watched herself with a new eye: her hips curvaceous, her waist slim, a perfect elongated navel making a deep and sensuous depression in her undulating stomach. Long and shapely legs culminated in the small triangle of black fuzzy hair, drawing her own gaze as well as his.

Unable to do anything to affect the outcome of

this bizarre occurrence, Ferne watched detachedly as the man fastened her ankles to leg rests. He swung these out so that her legs were parted widely. Another angled mirror on the ceiling showed her sex quite clearly, open enough for a man to thrust into it.

In the mirror she had watched him go about his business, his skin glowing on every muscle. From this viewpoint he was beautiful. Ferne's heart began to pound as the man worked round her, studying her as if she were a specimen in a display. She had never been looked at so blatantly. She had never felt so helpless.

When he moved to the foot of the couch she could see him in a wall mirror as he studied her between the legs. His expression was one of admiration as far as she could tell. Perversely it set up a quiver in her stomach.

Now he came to the head of the couch and bent low to her, the headiness of his scent swamping her again. As he put his lips to hers she breathed deeply, her mixture of fear and anticipation running high. It made her clitoris quiver.

The whisper of the deep and wooing voice made her tremble again. 'You are an exquisite woman, Cleopatra, and, even though you might fight to prevent it, I am going to make you come like you will never come again in all your life. So savour the moment. You will be in my debt for ever.'

'You'll never do it. I'll fight you every second until you give up and let me go.'

Ferne's heart thumped loudly in her tensioned

chest. The fear had turned to uncertainty, created through being helpless and by being told what she would or would not do. She had always controlled everything in her life. She had metered out her responses and given only as much as she needed to in order to get just what she wanted.

She disconnected now. Let him do his worst. Even though this man might think that he had control of her, he would quickly discover that she was made of tougher stuff than he thought. She would block him out, and just lie compliantly. He would get no response of any kind from her. And when he'd finished, she would walk away with her head held high, her pride intact. If Johnny thought he could have this man humble her, he was wrong.

'You are beautiful, Cleopatra, and I'm going to set you free.' The giant kissed her tenderly. 'And you are going to lick my balls in ecstasy and you will plead for me to let you have my cock. But even if you tear yourself apart to get it inside you, still I will refuse you. Do you hear?'

'You must be mad to think that I'd even consider it.' Despite her resolve to remain aloof, she automatically retaliated. It was in her nature and there was no other way she could keep any self-esteem.

'We will see.' He ran his finger lightly over her breasts, down her centre to her clitoris and back. 'I've had many women on this rack. At first, they all set out to defy me; to tell me that I would not rule them. But I tell you, Cleopatra, before another half hour is over, you will be screaming to be taken. You will agree to any price I demand of you.'

'Go to hell. Pig.'

He showed her a heavy plate of metal, six inches square and the thickness of his thumb. It was flat but had a prominent bump, like a nipple, on the underside. As he placed it on her lower abdomen, the small, sharp nipple pressed down on her, touching at a spot between her navel and her pubis. Then he placed a heavy weight on the plate. She felt the metal nipple digging in, pressuring her stomach with a tension of half pain and half delight. The depression in her lower abdomen pulled tightly at the skin of her pubis, tensioning her clitoris, pulling the diaphragms of skin around her labia tight into her groin.

As she looked with curiosity into the mirrors, she watched the man at the centre of the table, his black shaft springing as he wound a wheel. The table began to arch. The centre came up, and the arm and leg boards moved downwards. It was curving her like a bow.

At the leg section, he wound another handle. Her legs bent under from the knees, tightening the top surfaces of her thighs.

At the head he wound again. Her head went down, the skin of her neck taut. Now she was an arch, her stomach high above her shoulders, every inch of her skin tensioned by the movement of the table.

Her thighs were tight, their top surfaces pulling at her hip bones. Her arms also felt the pull, her armpits straining into taut hollows. She could see reflections of her rib cage clearly. Her breasts had disappeared into her chest, only the nipples standing proud. They had become super-sensitised now, erect and so taut that they hurt.

Now he moved the leg sections of the couch outwards, straining those webs of skin between her inner thighs and her secret lips. Those lips were tensioned upwards by the weight, and outwards by the splay of her legs. Her sexual mouth strained open widely, her clitoris standing proud as he racked her out.

She began to pant.

Her head went further back, her neck as tense as a leaf-spring, her hair falling freely over the end of the head-support.

Now the nipple on the metal plate pressed so hard it hurt her. Like the urge to urinate when it has been held too long, it ached in the pit of her abdomen. She tried to pee but she could not, having emptied herself earlier.

Now her heart raced. All her senses were alive, every millimetre of her body screaming with the tension. But he wound the table more. There was not an inch of skin on her body which felt as if it was not stretched to breaking point. Each nerve ending seemed to scream its sensation along a web of tiny fibres leading either to her nipples or to her clitoris. Her whole body began to tremor. But this caused the nipple on the weighted plate to goad her more.

Ferne felt like St Catherine, fixed backwards on a wheel, every muscle straining for relief.

As her stomach panted, the weight rose and fell,

making the nipple on its underside massage with excruciating pleasure-pain.

Her sex now spasmed, trying to shift the weight to relieve the pain to make the pleasure flow down and outwards through her swollen labia. Her clitoris was erect and pulsing like it had never pulsed before. She began to pant deeper.

Now with her head pointed backwards, an upside-down image of a pair of burnished legs came to her view. Above her face, the shaft loomed, striking up towards his athletic abdomen, his heavy testes hanging loosely just inches from her. Astride her head, he widened his stance and placed himself so that she could not quite touch the testicles with her tongue had she had a mind to do so. The strap at her neck would have throttled her had she overreached.

Now he wound her head support up so that her face came a half inch from his scrotum, but she could not move to bite him.

The sight of him so close, and more of the thick and stimulating scent of him in her nostrils, set her solar plexus trembling, intensifying the sensation from the weight.

'Now you will lick, my beauty. Lick my balls until I say you may stop. Then if you lick well, I will make you come. If you do not obey, I will keep you on the edge of ecstasy and leave you there until you scream for me to take you.'

'Go to hell.'

When he touched her nipples it was not a loving touch. He dug thumb and forefinger in at each side. Then he plucked them. They shrieked. A shudder went through Ferne's body, shaking the weight so that it pleasured her further, making her near to orgasm.

Now he ran his nails through the tightened hollows of her underarms. Her muscles tightened, pulling her arms tauter against the fastenings at her wrists. The nails slid on, to her breasts and from there to her navel. It left a trail of fire; thin and burning. She shuddered more, and again the weight on her lower stomach heaved, sending waves of pleasure-pain into her clitoris and sex. This began to spasm rhythmically. Desperately she tried to stop it all, but she couldn't. The man had taken over her body and was making it do things she would never have believed were possible. He was defying her most vehement refusal to submit to him.

Now she saw him take a long rod with a feather at the end.

He began to run it over her. First across the drum-tight stomach it went, then down the valleys beside her pubis. He touched so lightly that she could hardly feel it, but it set up a reaction which made her shudder again. The weight pressed harder, the sensations exquisite.

Reaching forwards, he laid the rod between her sex-lips, just touching her as he ran it up and down. Now she needed to orgasm, or to relieve the tension somehow. She didn't think she could hold out much longer and tried to contact the rod more fully, to open herself wider, straining the webs between her thighs as tight as they could go.

'Lick, Cleopatra, and I will consider letting your tension free.'

She licked, just being able to touch his scrotum with the tip of her tongue. The sensation made her tense more, her breath held tightly so that she didn't move the weight. She could hardly bear it now.

As she licked his testes, he lowered slightly so she could contact him better, but not so low that she could bite.

The shaft tightened, the tip of it swelling, purple as it engorged. And still he worked the feathered rod, drawing it up so that it tickled her clitoris. When she strained for greater sensation he withdrew.

'Bastard. Stop torturing me. I've licked your balls, now make me come, for God's sake.'

He set back his head and let out a laugh of triumph. 'Better, my sweet, but not good enough.'

Now he slid his shaft over her tongue, in long and steady strokes. She raised her tongue stiffly to the glans as it slid past, the whole ten inches slipping in her saliva, until her tongue tip reached his testes again. Then he drew back until she touched the glans once more.

He worked the feather harder as Ferne licked faster. She gasped with every tickling pass between her labia, straining her legs to give him open access. Now she began to moan, her tension near to bursting, but still unable to be released.

Carried away by the ecstatic blend of pain and pleasure which her position was creating, Ferne licked avidly. She needed to find that little bit of extra stimulation which would make her climax under her control, not his. If she was going to come, she would do it herself and be damned to him.

But, as if sensing her stratagem, he withdrew, the feather still working its devilish magic down the quivering surfaces of her loins and back through her groove.

She strained her tongue, but he kept himself just out of reach, and any movement of her head strangled her.

'Do you submit, Cleopatra?'

'No, you bastard. No.' She was crying now, tears pouring, mouth gasping, her tongue desperate for a contact which might just create that last bit of sensation she needed to orgasm.

He took another wand, fluffy at the end, and stroked her breasts, her navel, and her sex. Had she been able to, Ferne would have writhed at the fleeting touch, her nipples straining to be taken lovingly.

'Do you plead yet, honey? Ask me nicely and I will release you.' His free hand caressed her breast, ran through the sweat of her exertion to her navel and pressed in deeply.

She gasped. Then with the frustration she snapped.

'Fuck me, then, you bastard. Fuck me properly like a man would, and be damned. Or perhaps you're not a real man after all.'

He laughed loudly at her assertion and worked

his penis until it curved so tightly that the veins stood out. 'And what is this, my pretty maid, a broomstick?' Now he dragged the feather through her labial groove. 'Say "fuck me, master" and I might just let you feel this.'

Ferne was beyond resisting his game now. 'Fuck me, master,' she sobbed. With the tension in her body and the enormous charge of electricity building in her, she was almost bursting, but not quite.

As she trembled, the weight rode on the waves, amplifying the sensation of each tremor, almost beyond bearing.

Then she felt her arms released. Her legs and her neck were loosed, and the weight removed. He scooped her up and held her, limp in his arms, her head still down, her legs draped too. Now as he pulled her to himself, her arms found their way round the trunk of a neck. There, she hung on tightly, her body squashed to the ebony skin, the slickness of her perspiration sensitising every inch of contact.

One of his arms held her waist, a huge hand grasped her bottom, one long finger easing deeply into her anus. She wriggled on it, but she was helpless and the wriggling only served to intensify her need.

Now he turned her upright and held her to himself. He slid her down his trunk so that the tip of the great shaft just touched her secret lips. Another few millimetres and she could feel it just nosing into her.

'I've done what you asked,' she whispered.

'Take me properly now. Don't do this to me any longer.'

He just held her there, on the brink of penetration.

'That's good, Cleopatra. I have you in my power. I'm glad that you see how helpless you are. And I have the power to bring you to climax or to refuse you. I could crush the life out of you if I chose.' He squeezed gently so she would get the point.

'But I choose to love you. You are beautiful and I will not torture you more. Do you submit to me?'

She nodded her head.

'Say, "I submit to you, master. Do what you will with me." '

'I submit to you. Do what you will.'

'Master?'

'Master,' she whispered, with tears streaming down her cheeks.

And as she said the word, he lowered her on to himself, so gently that she hardly felt him slide. Now she was filled with him, hanging on his phallus, and on his finger deep inside her bottom. She was totally and utterly helpless; completely under his power. And she desperately needed to climax.

But as he held her tightly, moving her gently up and down on his shaft, she felt so small and insignificant. Her tension was still at an agonising height as she hung, impaled in the most intimate way that could be, and she gave herself up to him.

How many times had she tortured others? She had screwed some of them financially. She had wielded the power of money over them, keeping them in suspense while she decided the fate of the businesses they had spent their lives in building. Some had given themselves up to her and she had thrown them to the wolves, selling off their assets and leaving them with little more than memories and bitterness. She had been ruthless in the pursuit of what she had wanted. Before this time, she had submitted to no one. Now what would her mentor do with his power? What fate would he deal out to her? Would he simply cast her aside, leaving her to beg for completion?

Moving gently with her still impaled on him, he walked to the bed. The walking created wonderful sensations inside her and she wished he would continue around the room. But he lay on the bed on his back, with her on top of him so that she could feel his great length deep inside her.

As Ferne writhed, the unrelieved tension building again, he slid her steadily. She widened her legs, stretching herself, trying to recapture the tension of the rack. Now she gripped his neck and pulled and slid and heaved until, on his deeply thrust finger and his shaft, she came in a flood of aching, heating pain and pleasure; not explosively but so completely that the whole of her body seemed to swell with it.

As she wracked on him, at first in rigor then in glorious abatement of all her tension, he kissed her head and held her to himself. In his arms, his legs around her, his shaft and finger still intimately in place, he rocked her like a baby.

Ferne raised her head and looked up into his eyes. They were bright with triumph.

He grinned. 'Did you come nicely, baby?'

She kissed his chin. 'I came wonderfully. Did you?'

He shook his head. 'This is your time, honey, not mine.'

She raised herself to study him closely, the proud face looking back without a flicker of his eyes.

'What's your name?'

'You can call me Samson, if you like.'

She rested her cheek on the broad expanse of chest. 'Was I a pain, Samson?'

'No more than they ever are. Then they become addicted to the rack. It creates tensions which are not possible by any other means.'

'You can say that again. But I'm still not sure what this was all about. Wasn't it to break my will?'

He shook his head, his chest seeming to echo under her ear. 'No. Not to break your will.'

'But why did you make me submit to you that way?'

'That is for to you to decide.'

'You're very profound.'

'I have an honours degree in philosophy. Does it show?' He laughed a booming, hollow laugh.

'I think you're incredible.'

'And I think you are the most beautiful creature I've seen here for a long time.'

'I feel humble.'

'Don't. Hold your head high now. You were right to fight, but you have learned to submit. It can sometimes be just as valuable in life.'

She stroked his face tenderly.

'What can I do for you, Samson?'

'Would you allow me to make love to you?'

She slid upwards, giving her consent as she kissed him fully on the lips.

He turned with her, his shaft still penetrating her deeply. Holding himself over her so that none of his vast bulk bore down on her, he began to work himself slowly and gently inside her.

Ferne brought her legs up so that she was stretched widely for the great thickness of the black shaft. He pulled it out until he was almost clear of her, and then slid it back in to its hilt. She was amazed that she could accommodate such length and girth. And it was utterly marvellous to be taken by such a giant with such tenderness.

As his stroke speeded, becoming more urgent, she put her hands up to cup his face, and whispered, 'Fuck me, master.'

He smiled and worked her hard and long, still careful not to hurt her, still so gentle in the application of the rigid, ebony flesh. She felt every inch of it, the great testicles dragging between her legs, rasping at her loins, stretched this time because she wanted them to be.

With a gasp he pulled right out, laid the black phallus on her stomach and pumped.

A fountain of thick fluid shot over her breasts, reaching her chin, splashing her mouth. She licked it away as he put his head back, gasping as he rubbed his pouch over her pubic hair, his shaft gushing copiously, filling her navel with its emission. She worked her hands through it, anointing her breasts, her neck and her stomach. And then she slipped down under him until she could take him in her mouth. There she suckled him, drawing the last salty drops of his coming, letting him pulse warmly between her lips.

Then, with long and loving strokes, she licked his balls.

Chapter Eight

FERNE WALKED BACK to her London flat from the Underground station, dressed in a blue silk gown borrowed from Mai Lin. In the hot summer weather, she was naked underneath it and it made her feel wanton. Something in her wanted her to loosen the tie, fling the silk from her shoulders and run naked in the park.

Although alive from the experience with Samson, she was stiff with the strain her body had taken. She had fought him hard. She had fought the idea that she would ever succumb to his demands. Then, when he'd had her totally helpless and she had given in to him, he had become gentle with her. He could have crushed her. But he had overcome all her resistance, not with violence, but with the simplest of things – a feather.

It had been a lesson in the use of power. Now she did feel humble, but she didn't feel cowed, and as she walked with her head held high she didn't see the red Ferrari parked in the forecourt of the apartment block she owned.

It was the wonderful aroma coming through her door that made Ferne stop, her key still in the lock. Food? But her home help never left her anything hot.

Hunger drove its sharp pangs into her stomach. She had not eaten since a snatched salad sandwich at lunch.

Warily, Ferne opened the door.

Soft music by Richard Clayderman filled the air. It was the compact disc she had played in her car when Van Hagen had ambushed her at Capthorne Beeches.

She took stock quickly: soft lights. Two red candles; her best silver, shining in their light. White wine in a cooler. French bread. Cheeses: red and blue and soft white. A basket full of exotic fruit. Places set for two.

Then the smell came strongly to her: spices. Sweetness. Pungency. All were so appealing, it made her stomach rumble.

'Do you want to shower before we eat, darling?'

For a moment Ferne was sure that she was in the wrong flat. But the voice proved otherwise. A head of thick blond hair peeked around the kitchen door, the blue eyes twinkling wickedly. Elegant hands wiped themselves on her Egon Ronay apron.

She gaped.

'I hope you like Eastern food, Ferne. It's a bit of a mixture of Indonesian and Thai. I lived with an Indonesian girl and then a Thai girl so I got very good at a lot of things.' Van Hagen winked. Then he poured her a glass of red wine and offered it.

She glowered. 'What the hell are you doing in my flat, Van Hagen? I'll . . .'

He grinned. 'Your home help let me in just as she was going. I said I was the caterer for a party you're holding tonight.'

Ferne scowled. 'Well you can just take your things and go home – wherever that may be.'

He grinned again. 'I've just moved in down the hall and I haven't gotten any cooking stuff yet so I . . .'

Now she glared. 'You never give up, do you?'

He flashed his boyish smile, and crossed his arms. 'Your agent let the apartment next door to me. Didn't he tell you?'

She tapped her fingers on her arm. He looked raunchy with his sleeves half rolled, collar up, Presley-style. The blond hair fell casually over his forehead, the blue eyes sparkled, and his mouth seemed to call out 'kiss me'.

'I don't believe you, Van Hagen.'

He shrugged. 'Want to see my lease, neighbour? It seems that we're going to be seeing quite a lot of each other now that I'm a tenant of yours. My bedroom's next to yours. I hope you don't make a lot of noise late at night.'

'I'll have the lease cancelled.'

'It'll cost you a fortune in legal fees.'

'You're impossible.'

'So are you. But you look wonderful in that gown. It really suits you.'

Few people had ever said the little things to her which made her feel good. Van Hagen seemed to take the trouble to make her feel nice by noticing things about her.

'Flattery will get you less than nowhere, Van Hagen. Now if you'll take yourself out of my flat, I'll get back to my quiet evening at home.'

'I love you, Ferne.'

'Shut up.' She said it angrily but was already feeling uncertain of herself. What was it about the man that made her crumble?' He was a pain in the bum and an antagonist to her business plans. Why should she tolerate him? Now he had clearly moved into her block, just so that he could pester her more. She would give her letting agent hell in the morning. And her housekeeper.

He handed her the glass of wine, his eyes studying her face now.

She should have slung him out but she took the glass.

He sipped his wine, watching her steadily over the rim of his own glass as she slumped down in an armchair.

'Jan?'

'Yes, Ferne?'

'Jan, you really must stop this. It's getting to be . . .'

He came close. Too close. She was aware of her nakedness under the gown. All he would have to do to touch her intimately was to slip his hand through the folds.

'I agree that we must stop,' he whispered. 'It's getting to be a pain, sparring with each other all the time.'

'Jan, we must talk. We can't go on . . .'

'I know we must talk, Ferne. I've been trying to talk with you for years but you've shut me out ever since I went to the States. Why did you never answer my letters or my calls?'

Ferne felt very alone. The position which she had been bequeathed had become a burden which she was progressively less willing to bear. But she could not abdicate. Like royalty, the Daville dynasty must go on. But she needed someone to take a share, and someone to lean on at times. She needed to be held and cuddled and to be wooed for herself; not for the firm, or for her wealth. She had no one, and yet here was someone kneeling at her feet even though he was pestering her, playing games with her, wanting to make love to her, cooking her dinner, and being zany and witty and utterly charming. But she was fighting him every inch of the way.

He broke her reverie as he crouched beside her. 'Why didn't you ever reply to my letters or my phone calls, Ferne?'

'What letters?'

'The letters I wrote nearly every day for a year, stupid. And the calls which you were always too busy to answer. Why did you shut me out?' A note of hurt coloured his voice.

She pulled herself up straight, defensively. 'My father forbade me to have anything to do with you. He beat me after we'd been seen kissing in the summer house the night before you went away.'

'Christ almighty; why did you never tell me that?'

'I tried to, but your father wouldn't give me your address. My old man and yours hated each other for some reason.'

'If only I had known he'd beaten you, I would have come back and dragged you out of his clutches. But I thought that you had cooled.'

'I did when you got married.' She stuck her nose up petulantly.

'I only married after I had given up hope of marrying you. But because I was still in love with you, it didn't last long. Can't we try to take up where we left off?'

She turned away from him. 'I don't think so. That was such a long time ago. We've both changed so much. Besides that, I have my father's business to run. It takes all my time.'

Van Hagen stood up and paced and turned and paced again, finally turning on her with anger in his eyes. 'Hell, Ferne, you're twenty-five. Your old man is dead. Why are you still hanging on to his every wish?'

She stood and faced him. 'My father was a very wise man. He taught me everything I know.'

'He taught you to be cold and hard.'

She hit him so hard that his face snapped to the side with the force of the blow. He caught her arm and forced it backwards, his hand like a vice, stopping the follow-up blow.

'Let me go, Van Hagen. And get out of my flat.'

He shook his head. 'Oh no. I'm staying until I get some sense into that bigoted head of yours. You can scream all you like, I'll gag you and tie you if I have to, but by God, I'll make you see sense.'

Ferne wrenched her arm away and glared. Breathing heavily, she tried to still her racing pulse. Why was she behaving like this? He had made her mad again. His manner had been demanding, questioning her, pushing her for answers she did not want to think about. Until that last summer at the Beeches she had never believed that she could love anyone, or that anyone could love her for herself. Then she had fallen wildly in love with the young and brash son of one of her father's business rivals. She had almost died of sadness when he had been sent away. He claimed he had written, but there had been no letters or calls, and he was using that excuse to try to get back into her good books. But she needed Van Hagen in a strange kind of way even though she was suspicious that all he was after really was her money and to get control of Daville by the back door. And he was still after those shares to spite her and win the wager.

She wanted Johnny too, but he didn't want her for herself – only her fee. But that was all right. It had been a business deal and, when it was finished, she would be free of him and he of her: no obligations. No hanging on. Just a simple disconnection like she always did when she had got what she wanted from someone.

She looked at Van Hagen staring at her.

'I'm sorry. I'm just a bit tense, that's all. It's a bad time of the month.'

He laughed derisively. 'Don't give me that crap. Jees, Ferne, I'm not a child. I could always read you. You're tearing yourself apart over something. Now for Chrissakes spit it out or I'll take you over my knee and spank you.'

She smiled slightly as a wave of exhilaration went through her. He was being so masterful, almost like Samson had been.

'You wouldn't dare.'

She was draped over his lap before she could react. The gown was up around her thighs, her bottom in the air. Pummelling at his leg made no impression on his resolve to spank her.

'Van Hagen, I'll sue you for assault. You animal. Touch me and I'll . . .'

The first slap was light.

She wriggled.

The next was harder. Again and again he spanked her naked bottom, and as he spanked she felt herself coming alive. She felt his erection too, as it pressed against her pubis. She was molten. The stimulation of the session with Samson had been lurking shallowly under her anger.

She wriggled and got free.

He dived and caught her, and as he threw her on the settee, her gown came open, baring her torso and her breasts. Flinging himself on top of her to stop her running, he pinned her into the corner so she could not kick him. Then he kissed: her neck, her cheek, her lips. He was too strong and too passionate to resist. She didn't want to resist, anyway. After a token defence, she succumbed. She had learned how to succumb now, sensing that Jan Van Hagen would never hurt her.

Tongues fenced, lips chewed, necks got bitten and ears nibbled at. As Ferne wriggled and he took her mouth voraciously, his encumbered erection rode on her thigh. She wanted to grab at his zip to release it. She wanted to feel him deep between her legs, panting as he kissed her and kneaded her breast in his ardour.

To his annoyance, she pulled back, tore her arms free and pushed at him, her hot breath mingling with his, sliding into his open mouth and darting away again.

'No, Jan. We mustn't.'

'Why the hell not? You want me. I can see it in your eyes and by the way you kissed.' He bent and kissed her breasts.

She pushed him away again.

'You're wrong. Now, I think you'd better go.'

He shook his head. 'You haven't changed. You always were so damned scared to let me touch you – remember?' He shook his head again. 'Jees, what the hell did your old man do to make you so hard?'

Tears came to her eyes. She rubbed them away, tossed her hair from her face where it was stuck with perspiration. 'He beat me with a riding crop. He said that boys were dirty and that they were only after one thing.'

'That's true.'

'My money.'

'That's not true. I'm not interested in your damned money.'

'I don't believe you.'

'Believe what you like. I think you were brainwashed by your old man. But that doesn't mean you need to stay that way. You're the smartest girl I've ever met. You run rings round most men I know. You don't need all that crap about losing your money to greedy men.'

'All right. All right. Don't rub it in.'

'OK. But why are you giving me such a hard time?'

'You're still fighting me over those shares. You know I need the security for our loans.'

He closed his eyes with exasperation. 'I don't think we're ever going to see eye to eye over that.'

'You're still going to fight to keep control?'

'You bet your pretty fanny I am.' He stroked her naked pubis, and smiled.

Even though she covered herself, it made her thrill right through. But she could not and would not let him have her. She would not let him win.

As she tried to get up, he stopped her.

Again she thrilled, but fought it. 'I think you better go, Jan.'

'No, Ferne. I'm here for dinner, so just get used to the idea. Leave the damned business at the door and just be neighbourly for a little while.'

'All right, but only because you've taken such trouble over cooking dinner. You can stay to eat it, but that's all.'

He got up, looking down on her, his erection

standing strongly in his jeans. Aware of her moistness between her legs, and her pouting nipples, she wanted to fling wide the gown again and open her legs to him. She was past being Miss Prude. She was past being an iceberg. Right now she was melting again, but she could not give in to him.

Damn.

Ferne lay in the bath feeling full. The meal had been wonderful, the conversation light and amusing although she'd been alarmed when Van Hagen had said he was going away for some time.

She worked her finger over her vulva, letting the hot water rush up inside her, making her feel good. Her breasts floated fully as she opened her legs wider and closed her eyes, the tension in her lower abdomen building nicely.

The phone rang.

She picked it up with soapy fingers, smiling at the decadence of having a phone in the bathroom.

'Yes?'

'Hello, Cleo. How did you do today?'

'All right. I learned a lot.'

'Why are you whispering? Have you got a man in your bed?'

'No. He's gone. I'm in the bath.'

'Shame. I could have listened to you slipping and sliding over one another.'

'You're perverted.'

'I know. Isn't it marvellous being so uninhibited? So – are you sleeping with him?'

'No I am not.'

'Why not?'

'I'm not quite sure. Something keeps stopping me.'

'What?'

'I don't know. I think it's because I'm in love with you.'

'Don't be. You know there's no future in it. Go for the man you can get.'

'But, Johnny, you've taught me so much. I feel bonded to you.'

'You're bound to feel like that for a while. The first love is often compulsive if it works well. Now be a good girl and get into bed with Van Hagen. I'm sure it'll be all right.'

'Who said it was Van Hagen?'

'Ahh. Branching out are you?'

'The office boy, actually.'

'Paedophile.'

'The office boy's nineteen.'

'So you've developed a penchant for younger men, have you?'

'I was joking.'

'Of course. Now, are you going to have Van Hagen or not?'

'Why are you so anxious for me to jump into bed with him?'

'I'm interested to see how my student applies her study. And don't evade the question. Are you going to have him?'

'I keep sending him away, but he keeps on coming back again.'

'Seems that he's got more sense than I gave

him credit for.'

'Really. You're incorrigible.'

'Don't "really" me, Cleo. We're through the spoiled-girl bit. You're a woman now – an exquisitely sensual creature. Don't deny your feelings. Let yourself live. You don't have to marry the fellow.'

'I know I don't. But . . .'

'But what? Come on, you don't have any secrets from me. Remember, I know every follicle on your body and every bump inside you too.'

'Don't be coarse.'

'Shut up. What's your secret?'

'If it wasn't for being besotted with you, I might consider Jan. I loved him when I was eighteen, and I'm not sure that I've really stopped.'

'Well if you don't go with it, sweetheart, you'll never find out, will you?'

The line went silent for a while.

'I'll have to go, Johnny. I'm getting as wrinkled as a prune in here. When can we meet?'

'I don't know, Cleo. Would that really be such a good idea?'

'Please don't desert me now.'

'All right. I promise not to, just yet. Not until you see how things work out with this Van Hagen.'

'But when can we . . .?'

'I've arranged a lesson for you. The day after tomorrow. Three-thirty.'

'What will I learn?'

He laughed. 'In view of this conversation, I'll arrange something very special for you.'

They were a lonely couple of days, waiting for her next appointment at Mai Lin's.

Ferne had no man – no Jan or Johnny. She felt bereft. Trying to throw herself into her work she found it tedious. Meetings were boring. But people seemed pleased that she accepted their views and took their advice. She still held the final say over everything but seemed not to have to use it.

Robert was working hard with the brokers to get the final control of Van Hagen Enterprises. Even though they were friends again, she was not going to let Van Hagen win if she could help it. That was business.

By the time she reached Mai Lin's, she felt lethargic, not alive with expectation like the first time.

Mai Lin kissed her long and tenderly on the lips. She took Ferne's hand and led her to a room with easy chairs and a silken couch arranged in an arc around a fireplace. The rest of the space was covered with a large padded mat.

She turned anxiously to the oriental woman. 'What am I going to do, Mai Lin? I've stopped my period but I don't feel very sexy.'

'You still try to control everything, don't you, Cleopatra?'

'Perhaps I do. I wish sometimes that I could just let go. But . . .'

Mai Lin stroked her face and smiled. 'That will be all right Cleo. Today, you may just observe. Watch and learn and then apply what you learn when you have an opportunity. We are going to have some practical lessons. But first I have some things to do. While you wait, you may watch through this aperture.' Mai Lin drew back a curtain on the panelled wall to reveal a very small window. Then she left.

Ferne peered through the window and drew back quickly. Then she peered again. A young man and woman were in the room next door. The man was handsome, his eyes deep brown, his brown hair immaculately groomed. Well-cut jeans and a white shirt open almost to his navel gave him an elegantly casual air. Before him stood a large-eyed, black-haired girl, ample breasts hardly concealed in a tight tank top, revealing a sun-browned stomach, long and shapely legs showing beneath some skimpy shorts.

Within a few feet of Ferne, the young man traced the girl's breasts with his finger, running it up her neck to her lips. In turn she ran a long finger between his legs where Ferne could see a large bulge growing.

He kissed her tenderly and whispered in her ear. She giggled and did it again, running her fingers under him to cup him.

Ferne began to shake.

Then he slipped the tank top upwards, baring a pair of large and mobile breasts, nipples burgeoning strongly in dark brown rings of puckered flesh. Ferne wanted to suck them, just as she had sucked on Mai Lin's. But she looked on, mesmerised, still uncertain if she should withdraw or not.

As he opened the shorts, the girl put her head back and closed her eyes. Then she slipped out of them daintily, kicking them aside. She wore no panties, and as his hands ran down her flank and thighs Ferne had a full view of her mound. It was cleanly shaven away from her legs, just a quiff of black curly hair running down the centre. This acted like a guide for Ferne's eyes, leading them downwards into the deep central groove which divided the girl's sex.

Now his finger dipped into this groove and worked steadily. She widened her stance, her hands fondling her breasts. Ferne found her own hand slipping into her jeans and down inside her panties.

The young man stripped himself naked, displaying a slender organ, straight as a die, topped by a velvety knob. As he stripped, the shaft sprung slightly, his testes swinging. And as the girl cupped them, Ferne wanted to do that too.

His thigh muscles were firm, and his small bottom tightened as he pushed his shaft forward into the girl's palm.

Their mouths met, kissing deeply, their tongues flashing glossily. And between their bodies, his penis stood strongly, the tip of it grazing her stomach, the hairy purse rubbing on her mound.

Ferne wanted to push aside the young woman and usurp her place.

The girl slipped down the fine-haired chest, sipping at the small nipples, tonguing in his navel, until her mouth found his shaft. She closed her eyes and sucked.

Ferne swallowed reflexively.

Now only an arm's length away, the girl's mouth gobbled greedily, his thighs tensioned, his pubis thrust outwards. The shaft was glazed with her saliva as she mouthed it, sucking the skin right over its head, then plunging down again.

He pulled her up, and threw her over his shoulder. As he pivoted, she displayed her labia to Ferne. The valley of the lips ran right from her puckered secret hole, deeply dividing fully puffed-up lips. Ferne's own sex-lips tightened as she viewed it, her clitoris thrilling, her mouth going dry. My God how she needed to put her mouth to those lips and savour them.

As the young man held the girl over his shoulder, he opened her legs. Her sex opened too, the skin on each side of it stretching, the tongue of her clitoris poking out at Ferne.

Now he took her to the bed and laid her on her back, kneeling over her, his feet to her head. Ferne could see her sex wide open, glistening now with excitement and expectation. The girl craned up and took his phallus in her mouth as he dipped between her legs and licked her.

They worked avidly, he sucking at the distended labia while she took him deep into her mouth. Without disconnecting, they tumbled, she on top of him, his face buried in her, his tongue probing her deeply. She closed her eyes and drove down on him, her fingers stroking his testes, each stroke evoking a jerk of pleasure from between his legs.

Ferne stared as the brown-skinned bottom heaved, the cheeks opening and closing as he pulled them apart to access his prize.

The girl frogged her legs widely now, the puckered hole winking at Ferne as she kept up her voyeuristic appraisal of the scene, the girl's labia gliding over her lover's lips.

As Ferne watched, wide-eyed, they licked and stretched. Then they rolled again, he twisting until he was between her legs.

He bent her legs right back, straining them so that her knees touched her breasts, flattening them to her chest. Then the phallus dipped into her.

Ferne watched with fascination as it nosed between the fleshy lobes and disappeared. Still the testicles swung loosely as he moved. Now he had her open wide, his ramrod arms hooked in the crooks of her bent-back knees, her head lolling, and her eyes wide with lust. His pubis met the girl's, their hair mingling for an instant, before pulling out, then in, then out again. On the flats of his hands now, he hung over her, ploughing her, tensing the whole of his body as he strained his pelvis forwards and downwards.

When the orgasm came, Ferne watched the life-filled liquid overflow. She gasped and worked her finger frantically over her clitoris as the girl wracked on her lover. And then the couple fell apart, both on their backs, his penis throbbing. And the girl lay with her legs wide open, the glistening lips contracting gently, the tips of her fingers working at her nubbin.

Then they both sat up and grinned at Ferne looking through the peephole.

Ferne was flustered when Mai Lin came back. She was sitting on the settee scanning a magazine.

'Did you learn anything, Cleopatra?' Mai Lin's eyes searched Ferne's face deeply.

Ferne swallowed hard and nodded.

'Good. Now – I wish to see how well you have learned about how to handle men. If I am satisfied, I will give you a very precious gift.'

Ferne smiled. It sounded almost like Christmas. What kind of gift could it be? A vibrator? A videotape? A steamy session with Mai Lin or Mark?

Mai Lin smiled and rang a small brass bell. In response, the door opened and a young man entered. Oriental in his features, his brown eyes shone with pleasure at seeing Mai Lin. Ferne fancied that she even saw love there.

'This is Tang.' Mai Lin spoke a few words of a strange tongue and the young man bowed to Ferne. 'He knows no words of English. If you want to communicate anything, you will have to let him know your desires by gestures and touch alone.'

Ferne glanced up at Tang, the almond-shaped eyes looking on her kindly. He was dressed in a robe, and Ferne could not see his body, but from his neck and face she anticipated that he would be the same honey-brown all over.

'You may undress him.'

Ferne stared at Mai Lin.

'But he's only a boy. I couldn't.'

Mai Lin put up her hand. 'He is almost twenty.

And he is not a boy. He has great experience in pleasing women.'

Ferne looked away.

'Cleopatra, do you wish to fail your test?'

It was sharply said and Ferne felt like an errant schoolgirl. 'But Mai Lin, he's too young for me, and I'm too old for him.'

'He does as I command him, Cleopatra. Now, are you going to disobey me?'

Ferne was in a spin. This was so unexpected. She had thought that by now she would have learned all that she could. Now Mai Lin was posing another problem. Could she make love to the tender Tang?

'I do not ask you to make love with him, Cleopatra. You may wish to later, but for now, you have to demonstrate to me how well you have learned. Undress him.'

Feeling the sting of the reprimand, Ferne stood. Tang was almost as tall as herself. His face shone with pleasure as she looked into his eyes. The skin of his smooth and oval face had a marvellous radiance. Certainly he was at the peak of his virility.

She eased the young man's gown apart. Gently she slipped it off his shoulders, more muscular than she had imagined. He was slim and trim and tight and smooth. Unlike the smoothly shaven Mai Lin, he had a triangle of wiry black pubic hair although the remainder of his body was quite hairless. Ferne could not help tracing the fine curves with her fingers, running them down the centre of his chest. He was almost feminine in his smoothness and the grace of his curves. But muscles swelled under her touch. His hips were angular, his legs firm and strong. Between them hung a long brown penis, heavy testicles beneath it.

'Show me how to make him strong, Cleopatra.'

Ferne shot her a glance with a frown.

'Do not defy me.'

Ferne didn't dare. Also, she wanted to touch Tang. She wanted to experience him just as she had wanted to experience Mark. But still she doubted that she could have sex with him, or allow him to have her. There was something innocent about him that she could not put out of her mind.

Now she knelt in front of Tang, took his penis in her palm and lifted it to her cheek. With her nose against his groin she cradled him, scenting his spiciness, the warmth of his lithe body, the softness of the organ.

She kissed it at the root where it joined his pubis, closing her eyes, working it very gently with her fingers. It was a moment before she felt it stir. She breathed heavily now, knowing that she was under examination.

As he grew to her touch, Ferne kissed the underside and as he stiffened and reared in the warmth of her fingers, the head emerged as if stretching and waking from a long sleep. She kissed the web of skin at the division of the head and drew a deep breath of his scent, more musky as the foreskin unfurled.

It was now strong and growing rapidly between her fingers, and she turned him so that he had his back to her. Her hand slipped through his legs and cupped his testicles, the first and middle fingers yoking the hardening shaft, pulling it downwards so that the foreskin stretched tightly above.

She felt him pulse and thrust forward slightly, and was pleased that she was creating pleasure for him.

Mai Lin sat and smiled at her, but took no notice of Tang's demeanour.

Now with a palm full of man's most prized possessions, Ferne wound her other hand around the waist and took the tip of the growing shaft between her thumb and forefinger. She rubbed gently, each movement causing a small spasm as her cheek rested naturally against his flank above the hip. He felt so warm and strong as she hardened him.

Now, when she released him and turned him to face her, Ferne was surprised at the enormous size he had grown to. Rigid and curved, springing away from the tight abdomen, he was as potent as any of the men she had handled, apart from Samson.

Now she took the virile Tang deep into her throat, her tongue exploring the hollow groove which ran the length of the shaft and culminated in the deep division of the glans. She sucked up, pulling the foreskin tightly over the head before driving it down with her lips again, just as the girl next door had done.

'Very good, Cleopatra. You may let him go now. If you wish, you may finish him later with your mouth or hand, or you may take him into yourself. He is very strong and he has youthful vigour. My trainees are all kept on Chinese herbs which make them very potent. You will be surprised just how much they can ejaculate at one time. If you keep a man on such herbs, he will please you greatly until he becomes quite old.'

Ferne studied Mai Lin with fascination. It was as if she was speaking about a dog or a car, or something one possessed.

Mai Lin smiled. 'I can see you have learned well, Cleopatra. If you handle your man as well as you handled Tang, you will have a happy one. But you must also allow him to fuck you. Men don't like being brought by hand too often. Some like you to suck them, but many like to finish inside you. You will find that for many men, entering you from behind is their most favourite. It is what they were designed to do. Most animals make sex this way.'

Again Ferne was bemused. This was the most practical lesson she had had. At school the subject of sex had been reduced to reproductive biology and immersed in sniggers.

'Now, you have aroused your man, or perhaps he is horny simply by looking at you. How are you going to stop him taking you should you not desire it?'

Ferne looked at the rampant young man and then at her mentor. Apart from kicking and scratching, she didn't know.

'Very well, we will teach you some simple defence. Tang will attempt to enter you, and you must prevent him from doing so. Take your clothes off.'

Reluctantly Ferne stripped off her clothes, feeling strangely shy before the young man. His eyes appraised her body with apparent admiration, and she fancied that his erection became perceptibly harder.

Now they faced each other on the padded mat, Mai Lin sitting sipping tea as she watched them.

'Tang is going to attempt to fuck you now, Cleo. Try and stop him.' She gabbled words of another language at Tang.

Ferne's heart leapt. For one thing being attacked by a man had always been a fear of hers.

As Tang advanced, Ferne took up a defensive position, her fingers clawed outwards. The next few moments were a nightmare. He took a finger and twisted it. She went down on her knee to avoid the pain. He plunged her to the mat and had her legs open in a trice. But then he withdrew, leaving her like a stranded turtle, her legs splayed widely as he smiled down at her swollen labia. Under his appraisal, she felt them pulsing strongly, despite her anger at being bested by a youth.

Ferne glowered and sprang up.

The next time he came at her, she kicked out. This was also fatal. He took the foot, twisted and pulled and had her on her stomach in a trice. This time he came down on to her back with all his weight, an arm bent up behind her.

She felt the warmth of his strong erection in the crevice of her bottom. Then, with one skilful move he was deep inside her despite her struggling. She gasped at the force of it.

But again, he withdrew.

The next hour proved crucial in Ferne's training. Naked too now, Mai Lin taught her carefully how to combat attacks from all directions. Ferne quickly learned how to defend herself against a knife, and how to disarm her attacker. By the end of the period, she was feeling much more confident. But she was much more stimulated too.

Close combat with Tang, their naked skins touching as they wrestled, his penis rubbing at her thigh, her secret place slipping on his leg, all conspired to make her horny. But still she could not imagine herself making love with him.

They practised some more, Ferne now much more determined not to be beaten. Most times, Tang overpowered her easily, once pinning her on to her back and entering her deeply but briefly. She thrilled as she felt his strong shaft driving between her vaginal walls. Her breasts were tight against his smooth skin, her labia swollen with the excitement of the chase and capture.

The next time, she overcame him and had him at her mercy. She could have damaged him for life had she wanted to.

Mai Lin stood astride Ferne as she lay beside Tang, panting. Ferne looked up at the woman's naked sex, wanting to raise herself and put her mouth to it. But Mai Lin was clearly not offering herself that afternoon.

'Good. You have learned well, Cleopatra. Now,

would you like to finish Tang with your mouth, or open your legs for him?'

Ferne shook her head and sat back.

Mai Lin must have seen her doubt. 'Very well. Would you like to borrow him?'

Ferne was aware of her mouth dropping.

Mai Lin knelt with an amused expression on her face, working Tang's phallus almost absent-mindedly. It was the way anyone else would stroke a cat or fondle a dog's ears.

'I don't know what you mean, Mai Lin.'

'Do you want to take him home with you? I can only spare him for one week, but it will give him some experience.'

Ferne's mind raced. She flushed brightly as Mai Lin continued her gentle masturbation, Tang's pelvis thrusting forward now. She slapped his leg and spoke sharply. Ferne assumed he was getting a telling-off for being too forward or too eager to climax.

'What would I do with him, Mai Lin? I'm out at work all day.'

'He will amuse himself. He can cook well and he is very good about the house. You wouldn't know he was there until you wanted him. You may practise all you have learned here. He is very obedient. He will do anything you could desire a man to do.'

Chapter Nine

TANG HELD FERNE'S hand as they walked towards Knightsbridge. She felt like his aunt. His sister. His mother, even. But she did not feel like his girlfriend or lover.

In Harrods his eyes were wide with astonishment when she bought him a personal compact-disc player. The choice of discs was his own, and she stood with pleasure and amusement as he listened to them, his brown eyes full of wonder.

She bought him clothes, replacing a simple cotton shirt and jeans with garments more suited to a young and wealthy man-about-town. Revelling in every minute of her giving, she wanted to show him that she liked him very much.

Because she was afraid that he would be bored while she worked, they combed the electronic-goods shops for hand-held games. He was fast. She was left in wonder at the speed at which he mastered them.

Proud of her escort, they stepped out of a taxi at her apartment block.

'This is Tang, George,' she told the doorman, who smiled at Tang dutifully. 'He'll be staying with me for a week. I want you to look after him and help him if he needs anything.'

'Of course, Miss Daville. Anything you say.' The doorman looked at Ferne askance but she took no notice. Let him think what he liked.

In the lift, Tang stood close to her. It seemed natural. There was nothing about him that scared her, even though she was uncertain about her feelings towards him.

They ate the reheated remnants of Jan Van Hagen's cooking. Tang seemed pleased that she had food he knew.

When she came into the living-room he was seated, his gaze glued to the television, flicking through the channels with the remote control. Everything seemed so new to him, and so exciting.

It was a nice experience to have someone she liked in her apartment and she felt radiant under his undemanding admiration, happy to be able to return something of it to him.

As bedtime approached, butterflies began to flutter in her abdomen. She showed him his room, gave him towels and soaps and a new toothbrush, demonstrated his shower, and pulled back his duvet for him. He stood smiling at her, but as she kissed him on both cheeks and withdrew to the door, a puzzled look clouded the almond face.

Ferne snuggled down, switched out the light and pulled her giant teddy close. It seemed so long already since Johnny had called, and Jan had gone away. She was dozing when she felt a breath of cool air. The warmth of the naked body which slipped in beside her made her thrill.

Tang cuddled up to her. She took him in her arms and held him close, stroking his face with her thumb. They slept like brother and sister, their nakedness unremarked, the softness of his penis and pouch against her thigh comforting without being stimulating.

In the morning, Ferne woke at six, surprised to find the naked, honey-skinned youth standing over her with a cup of tea.

Her eyes were drawn to the flaccid organ between his legs, long and curving, his testes swinging loosely as he moved.

'Hello, Tang. Is that for me?'

He smiled, handed her the cup and knelt beside her.

As she drank, he watched her, every little movement noted by the clear eyes. It was if he intended to learn everything he could from her.

When she got up, he pulled back her duvet. When she showered he followed her in and soaped her. Together they stood in streams of prickling water, his hands working lovingly over her breasts, her back, her bottom, and between her legs.

Kneeling, he looked up at her as he towelled her dry, his hands around her thighs, dabbing and patting at her sex-lips, her stomach and then her breasts.

Ferne sighed.

She felt loved. She felt privileged. Servants had always been a part of her life but she didn't think of Tang as a servant. Neither could she think of him as a lover. He was just Tang. Attentive, tender, admiring Tang. And he was totally uninhibited.

He fastened her bra, after seeing that she was comfortable in it. She smiled as he rummaged in her lingerie drawer and pulled out a pair of full, silk knickers. Frowning, he cast them aside and delved until he came up with a black lace thong she had been given but had never worn.

Grinning widely with satisfaction, he held it out to her so she stepped elegantly into it. Thrilled with the charade as he arranged it so it was comfortable in her crotch, she was drawn to him as he stepped back to admire it.

He knelt and set the triangle straight as if it was wrinkled.

She thrilled to the touch on her mound, but still held herself in check.

'Thank you, Tang. That feels very comfortable. I think you have great taste in women's underclothes.'

He smiled, clearly picking up the tenor of her compliment.

In the mirror she could see her wiry pelt through the lace and it made her feel sensuous. She smiled as she imagined walking through the office like this.

Gesturing to her to sit, Tang blow-dried her hair, and brushed it gently until it shone. It flowed around her face, springy and alive.

Ferne felt springy too.

She turned, reached up and touched his face with a gesture of thanks. Then she found a flowing skirt, with a pretty green floral print which she had bought in Paris the year before and had never worn either. A pale green blouse of finest silk, her diamond necklace fastened by Tang, and she was ready for the office. Today she would surprise them, her casual elegance contrasting strongly with her usual, formal suits.

Tang served her toast and coffee. He boiled her an egg and cut the bread into soldiers which was something she'd not had since she was a child.

At the door, she kissed his cheeks, one and then the other. Still naked, he held his face to her mouth for longer than she wanted. Then she was gone, striding down the corridor with lightness in her heart and in her step.

'I think we're going to strike out on those last shares, Miss Ferne.' Robert Trenchard looked grey and tired as he handed her her agenda for the day.

She grimaced at the list. It seemed so tedious. 'What's the problem with the shares, Bob? Can't you locate them?' Ferne sat back in her chair. All she could think of was Tang's naked body against her own.

Robert sighed. 'The broker's playing cagey. He's not sure if the holder will sell to us. My guess is that Van Hagen is offering more.'

'How much are we talking about to secure them?'

'About ten thousand over the market price, I should guess.'

Ferne sat back and tapped her blotter. Ten thousand over the market value was a lot to pay to get control of Van Hagen Enterprises. But she had sworn to do it. Heck, she had spent ten thousand on her tuition. Also, she had bet Jan Van Hagen ten thousand more that she would win control. The money seemed to have been spent either way. If she got the shares, it would cost her ten thousand. If she didn't get them she would still have to pay out the same amount on the bet. The one thing she still did not like was being beaten by the man, even though she wanted him. But she had forgotten something. Should she win, Van Hagen would pay her. She smiled. That would pay for her tuition. What an irony.

Ferne thumped the desk, her eyes shining. She must have the shares. That way she would beat Van Hagen at his little game and get control. He was at her mercy. She could have him or reject him at her whim.

'Go for it, Bob. Get the shares even if you have to pay over the top for them.'

Robert shot her a bemused look as she grinned. 'Can I share the joke?'

'Not really, Bob darling. It's private.'

He looked surprised and she suddenly realised what she had called him. But he was a darling. He had been more of a caring parent to her than her domineering father had been, and she loved him for it.

As he got up to leave, he turned. 'You're looking more beautiful than I have ever seen you, Ferne, my love. I'm so happy for you.'

Ferne thought she saw a tear as he turned away.

Tang looked even more sexy dressed only in a pair of her very short beach shorts. He smiled and kissed both her cheeks as he greeted her at the door. Thank goodness she'd sacked the cleaner for letting Van Hagen in, or news of the naked young man in her flat would be widely spread by now.

'Hello, Tang. How was your day?'

His brow creased. She gave him a reassuring stroke on the cheek and went through to her bedroom. She wanted to relax in a hot bath and soak away the tension of the day.

Turning on the taps in her bathroom, she found Tang beside her, naked. He put some herbal bath salts in the water, searching through her cabinet to see what else he could find. As he stretched upwards, his penis hung long and supple, his skin glowing in the light. She wanted to touch him, but she stopped herself. It wasn't right.

When he undid her buttons, she allowed him to remove her blouse, to slip down her skirt and run his soft hands over her shoulders. Her head went back at the touch, and she kissed his fingers. As he slid her bra straps down and undid the front clasp, the cups dropped away slowly. His eyes lit as her breasts came out and hung full and tense. Two long fingers traced the circles of her nipples and then slid down to her thong.

He knelt, peeled away the triangle of lace and kissed her pubis. Ferne shuddered with the pleasure that it brought between her legs.

Taking her around the shoulders and under the knees, he held her over the bath, his skin warm on hers, her nipples rising. She was surprised at his strength and control.

Carefully now, he immersed her in delicious heat, her breasts buoyant in the clear water, no bubbles to clothe her. But why should she need clothing from his eyes? She was open to his gaze and to his ministrations, whatever they might be. Since he had arrived in her flat, those ministrations had been kind and tender. Would they change when he became aroused? Would he turn into a rearing young stallion and take her against her will?

Naked, he stood over her, that limb she had held asleep now. It still hung, the purple head almost eclipsed by its supple, fleshy hood. The imp in her wanted to put out a hot hand and touch him. It wanted to wake the serpent and make it rear. It wanted to weigh the eggs and watch as they retracted for safety inside the ample folds of their wrinkled purse. She wanted to see the limb as stiff as iron but she could not summon the courage to do it. He looked so vulnerable.

Still he had not uttered even a word of his own language since they had left Mai Lin's. This kept an air of mystery between them. It intensified the tension in the atmosphere too as hot, wonderfully relaxing minutes ticked by.

Words sometimes spoiled an atmosphere. They were often the wrong words, or words which the other person did not want to hear.

Ferne watched through a haze, both of steam and her own euphoria, as Tang explored the bathroom. He found a bottle of baby oil, smelled it, and touched it. Then he went out silently. When he came back he poured something from a small vial into the baby oil. The aroma was powerful, a deep note of sandalwood blended with heating spices. The high tones of ylang-ylang? The headiness of neroli? It went to her head, producing pressure in the centre of her forehead. Vibrant warmth spread through her body with every stimulating breath. Slowly it seeped downwards, creating tingling in its wake until it reached the inner surfaces of her thighs.

Tang glanced down upon her and smiled. She was mesmerised by that smile. She was sure it showed in her eyes and on her face. And those dark eyes of Tang's could hood with such seduction that they would draw her attention across the room, unable to deny them. He knew it very well. He was clever in the way he used it. He was an Adonis in his looks, a Paris in his grace. And as he stood anointing himself, he was a Pan. She could imagine him running through dappled woods and silvan fields, the slender phallus standing proud like its owner, head up and erect.

Of course he was pleased that she was watching him. It was clearly a performance to arouse her.

As she watched, he turned and studied her, smiling lovingly.

She returned the smile, drawing him with it back to her side.

Kneeling at the head of the bath, Tang slid soapy hands over her shoulders. She put her head back, chin upwards, to give him full access, closing her eyes and sighing. He yoked her neck from both sides, and swept down along her shoulders.

Further downwards, his fingers found her breasts, lightly afloat, the nipples pouting with the heat of the water and the tension of an anticipated caress. Her breasts felt so firm under his touch as he encircled them, and lifted them, letting them rise and fall. The seduction of his fingers as they massaged her nipples made Ferne push out her breasts spontaneously towards him, each nipple wanting to feel his mouth now.

Unbidden, her body arched, her throat moaned in the quietness.

That task completed, Tang trailed a finger between her legs. It travelled lightly, skimmed between her love-lips, over her pelt, moving to her navel, until it reached her breasts again. Every touch set her senses trembling.

At each nipple he lingered, described little circles of sensation around it several times before tugging it into stiffness.

Again she pushed upwards.

This time he lowered his face, his tongue caressing a nipple, his mouth sucking the whole nimbus too. Then the kisses went to her neck, forming a succession of delicious shivers, upwards until he reached her ear.

'No, Tang, you mustn't. We mustn't. It isn't right.'

But she had forgotten that he spoke no English.

Ferne smiled and moved his fingers away from her. He looked puzzled. She stroked his hand. She had been melting under his caresses which had sent her into an euphoric bliss.

Without asking her permission, Tang lifted her from the bath, laid her in a nest of soft pink towels on the carpet, and began to pat her dry.

Ferne put back her head. She closed her eyes and let herself be pampered. She allowed herself be taken back to childhood.

The seductive touching of the towel reached her legs. She opened for him obediently, allowing him to pat dry her most intimate places.

Her mouth was open, her eyes shut when he kissed her forehead, then her cheeks. At first she felt the warm air of his breath sidling up to her face. But she moved her head to avoid his mouth touching hers, smiling reassurance as the face showed puzzlement.

Ferne's heart was racing. The inner surfaces of her thighs burned. She could feel the extra sensitivity of the secret lips, engorged by the stimulation of his presence.

She sighed.

Now he knelt beside her, pouring oil on her stomach.

From her navel, his finger tips made slow and sensuous circles, spreading outwards like ripples in a pond. Her abdomen rippled too.

He kneaded deeply, under her rib cage so that she had to catch her breath, the aromatic vapour coursing up her nostrils, and through her head.

Between her navel and her pubis he pressed, one finger plunging deep until she was taut. The pain of it made her gasp, her clitoris coming alive. Some kind of stimulation point?

The long, wise fingers encircled her breasts, raising them and caressing them until they became firmer. The oil seemed to tighten her skin, and her nipples became so hard.

Then he turned her, and straddled her, his penis between the valley of her bottom, his testicles nestling between her thighs.

For a moment she thought that he would take her that way, like Mark had. But as she felt the fingers splaying and closing and splaying again as they travelled down her spine, she smiled and closed her eyes.

What if he did take her? It would be his decision, not hers.

Shoulders, flanks, bottom, thighs, and hollows of her knees, all had their sensual attention. Her feet too, as he sat on his haunches working at the soles, between the toes, the ankles and on upwards.

Around her thighs the thumbs came, the fingers outside. Deep between the cheeks of her bottom they delved, finding succulent moistness there. She widened to give them access, too aware that she had become deliciously aroused by the slow and gentle seduction of experienced fingers and the aromatic oil.

Plunging downwards through the valleys between her labia and her inner thighs, he worked slowly and methodically. He didn't enter her, nor did he run his fingers through her groove. He simply massaged her intimately and then left.

When he turned her on her back again, his eyes shone down on her, his mouth smiling his satisfaction as he stood, and took her hands, pulling her to her feet.

Ferne stood before him, humbled by his gentleness and his kindness. In all this time he had not become erect.

By the finger tips he led her to her bedroom, and draped her in her robe. He dried and brushed her hair and took her to the dinner table.

A cold meal of meats and vegetables, of spicy rice and prawn crackers was followed by exotic fruits and ice cream. He must have taken most of the day to prepare it.

They sat together watching television, sipping wine and giggling at an old film, something Ferne would never have done on her own. She rarely sat down, let alone spent an evening relaxing like this.

In bed they held each other tightly, her arms around him, his hand stroking at her face.

The next days passed in the same way: the morning tea, the shower, the dressing and brushing of her hair. In the evening the bath, the massage and the meal. In bed they cuddled, Tang not making any attempt to take her, she not wanting to let him go.

Ferne could not wait to get home from the office

each night. She put off evening appointments, cleared her desk by five and was out of the building before the others had gone.

She felt alive and loved and cared for.

Only two days more and then Tang must go back. Mai Lin had been strict about it. She had arranged the time for Ferne to deliver him.

As the time wore on, Ferne felt herself becoming tense. She had grown to love her house-boy and knew that she would be heartbroken to lose him. Would he be sad to leave her? Perhaps she could persuade Mai Lin to let her keep him.

The meal that night was slow, both of them taking their time. The bath and the marvellous massage had been slow too. It was as if Tang needed to spin out his time with her, and she allowed it.

Sadness instead of joy filled his eyes each time he looked at her. Ferne felt sad too. Something was wrong, but she couldn't ask him. His time was almost up. Was he becoming aware that he must go back to Mai Lin?

As they sat on the settee with coffee, Tang snuggled close. He had followed her around the kitchen like a dog, nuzzling her at every turn. His games machines seemed not to interest him any more. He didn't play his CD player. The vitality she had loved seemed to have gone out of him.

In bed she held him close. She rocked him and kissed his forehead. He wound his arm around her waist, the hand resting under her breast but not holding it. He never touched her breasts or between her legs in bed. But he held on to her tightly.

She caressed his arm and his back, his strong, lean buttocks and his thigh. He was beautiful and his sadness made her cry inside.

'Tang, what's wrong? Have I hurt you? Is having to leave soon tearing you apart like it's tearing me?'

He snuggled closer, like a child which was frightened and had come into bed for comfort.

She raised herself on her elbow and looked down into his eyes. She smiled, but got no smile in exchange. Instead, a tear burgeoned and ran down the perfect, brown cheek.

'Oh my God, Tang,' she whispered. 'What's wrong? What must I do to bring that light back into you?'

Instinctively she lowered her lips and kissed his mouth. It was fleeting but it brought a glimmer of pleasure. Again she kissed, lingering longer, feeling the succulence of the full lips, breathing in his musky body scent.

He smiled.

Her heart leapt.

Suddenly she knew. He wanted to be loved. All week long he had been loving her in his way and apart from her gifts and her acknowledgements she had not returned it. She had been afraid. She had treated him as a boy. But he was a human being. He had cleverly hidden his feelings. He had not become sexually aroused. He had not touched her sexually, except in the bathroom as part of his nightly service.

She put her arm around his shoulder and kissed him long and tenderly.

His mouth responded. She felt him stir. Her hand wandered lightly over the taut chest, smooth with the body oil, stimulating with its aroma.

He shuddered as her hand found his penis. As she held it, it slowly grew. She fondled it, pulling the skin up gently and working it down very, very slowly.

As he grew in her hand, his body stiffened. He took a deep breath and pushed out his pelvis. His eyes closed, and when they opened, the light was back, the mouth smiling.

'Fuck me, Tang.' These words he knew, and they acted like a magic spell.

Under her gaze the boy changed into a man, the light of love turned to playful wickedness. He knew what she wanted of him. He had needed her permission.

Taking her around the neck, he pulled her mouth on to his. The kiss was so long and so deep and so passionate, it made her gasp. Only Johnny had kissed her like this.

Then he rolled her, hanging over her, his hand gripping her neck hard from behind, his mouth bearing down on her mouth, open to receive his darting tongue.

The hand moved to her breasts. It lifted and pulled and kneaded as usual but this time with the intent of arousing her.

Now the hand performed its massage and travelled in small pressing circles until it dived between her legs. She opened to it as it took her nubbin and slipped through her lips and dug deep into the hollows of her loins.

Then he slid down her, his mouth taking her nipples one by one, pulling and releasing and sucking them up so that she arched with the delight of it. At her navel he probed, and then sank between her legs, the tongue finding her swelling clitoris, teasing it into life.

His hands were under her knees now, pushing her open, forcing her knees to touch her breasts. She was exposed and stretched as he took her sex-lips with such ardour that she shuddered at every suck and lick and playful bite.

'Oh my God. Ohhhh.'

When he came up, he came like a steam piston, his phallus driving straight and true and deep. Into her he slid, and took her. He pivoted on his hands, his hips swinging like an athlete doing press-ups, his shaft driving into her with such unerring power that she rocked with the force of it.

His eyes shone. His body glistened with the sweat of his exertion and Ferne cried out with every thrust.

She'd been a fool. She had denied him the ultimate pleasure of pleasuring her. He had deemed himself to have failed in his duty to Mai Lin.

Tang began to pant and exclaim with every thrust. They were the first words she had heard him utter.

Ferne raised her legs. She grappled his hips and swung them forward on the in-stroke, pushed them out as he pulled away.

He grinned, his eyes flashed, his shaft drove deep and long, each time almost coming right out of her before boring deeply again.

She wound her legs around him, she scratched at his back with her nails, the tension in her building to a climax.

When she came with a flash of lightning in her head, red and blue and gold stars seemed to spin in a void of blackness, darts of light rocketing as the pain of pleasure ripped up through her breasts and into her cheeks.

He tore himself out of her, slid up her body, his pouch richly lubricated with her nectar, his phallus gleaming.

He pushed between her breasts, pulling them together to form a valley for his shaft, his back arched and his head straining backwards. And as he thrust his pelvis forwards, driving through her cleavage, he ejaculated in a spurt so strong it covered her neck and splashed over her lips, her face and hair. Pumping strongly, he filled the space between her breasts.

Now he pinned her hands above her head and bore down on her breasts, prolonging the dying feelings of his orgasm by sliding though his semen, making her breasts alive with its slippery texture.

His passion spent, he massaged her, just as he had done with the oil. He worked his fluid into her stomach, over her cheeks, her throat and her lips.

Ferne squirmed at the lasciviousness of the act.

Now he turned, straddled her face with his phallus still ticking. And she reached up and lapped him, savouring the saltiness of his scrotum, raking his shaft with her tongue.

He licked her too, between the legs, and sucked her. He rasped at her clitoris, already rising in interest again. And when satisfied with his work, he turned again, pulled her up and took her mouth with a fervour hardly diminished from the first kiss.

Under the onslaught, Ferne writhed. This man was a demon lover. He outmatched and outpaced any of the lovers she had had so far. What a fool she'd been.

As he pinned her hands above her head, he came into her again. She moaned with the slow and thorough pace of it. Bending his head he took a nipple and sucked. The combination brought fire to her nubbin and she wriggled on him, desperate for force.

From under her pillow he produced a vibrator, ran it over her breasts as he sat back, his shaft still in her. Then, when he pushed the vibrator between her legs to titillate her clitoris, ripples of pleasure waved over her. It brought her to another climax so quickly she was amazed.

This time he came inside her, the hot flush of his semen sensitising her, making her writhe with the pleasure of it.

Gently he continued to work her, until she subsided in a languor, spent of all the energy she had imprisoned over the past days with him.

They kissed and hugged, and slipped on one another. They touched and pulled and rubbed and slid their hands over her breasts and nipples and his penis and his testicles. And when the floating warmth of their exertions had faded, he carried her to the shower.

This time she showered him, soaping him, and running her fingers into his cracks and crevices, exploring his forbidden places. She sucked on him lovingly, and took his testes in her mouth, careful not to hurt him, thrilled at the trust he lent her.

They suppered late and drank white wine and ate cracker biscuits with cheese, feeding one another, stealing food from each other's lips.

Then they danced into the early hours of the morning hugging closely to gentle rhythms before they went to bed. Tang turned himself and slept with his face between her legs, his mouth to her secret lips, kissing while she took his penis in her mouth and suckled on him like a child with a comforter.

And in the morning he brought her tea.

It was the last day. My God, it was their last day. She had to take Tang back by six that evening.

Frantically Ferne phoned the office and left a message for Robert. She was sick. Please handle all her appointments. Make whatever decisions he thought fit.

Tang and Ferne breakfasted. They lounged naked on the settee, she with her hand between his legs, his arm around her neck.

Afterwards he left her, went to his room and brought back a book. Where he had got it from she did not know.

She gasped at the contents of raw sex in all its variations, sharply shot in brilliant colour.

He thumbed through the pages, watching her face intently as she focussed on each set of lovers, each huge shaft of man-flesh and every voracious sexual mouth.

'My God, Tang. We're not going to do . . .?'

He grinned and pointed to one picture. She had taken a second look at it already and he had picked up her interest. It was something she had not experienced in all her learning so far.

She shot him a look of mock horror and backed away.

He smiled knowingly and moved towards her.

She got up.

He advanced.

She giggled and he let out a laugh of lust, his eyes sparking with it, his shaft already stiff.

They sparred; adrenalin running through Ferne like fire coursing through her veins. He chased her around the furniture as she giggled like an adolescent.

He grabbed her and she escaped. But now he cornered her, dived into her waist with his shoulder, lifted her and hoisted her.

Ferne wriggled. She beat his back. She grabbed the settee to stop his mad career towards the bedroom. They toppled and sprawled in a heaving mass of arms and legs before he broke free and caught her arms, dragging her across the carpet like a sack of potatoes.

'No, Tang, no.' She wriggled and kicked and

squirmed and fought him, but he was too strong for her. He was marvellously, and uncontrollably strong. He dominated her at each turn, and she loved every minute of it. The soft and loving servant had turned into a whirlwind of masculine force that was taking her off her feet. His virility and his strength astonished her.

Now he threw her face down on the bed, her knees on the floor, just as the picture in the book had showed her. Then bearing down into the small of her back to stop her rising, he spread her legs widely with his knees and drove straight into her.

Ferne took a long sharp breath as the root of his shaft rammed up against her secret place, setting waves of excitement raging through her. It seemed to connect with her clitoris and her nipples, bringing her vaginal walls into spasm almost immediately.

Then he moved his hands to her buttocks, spreading her wide for his thrusting, his thumbs digging in hard beside her anus. And as he thrust he let out little moans of joy. Now his thumb was invading that small hole, and as he drove it deeply into her, the pain of it was wonderful.

Ferne moaned, 'Fuck me, Tang. Oh my God that's too beautiful.'

When she came, she flooded, and he pumped again, and they rolled and they laughed and each thrust a leg between the other's legs, revelling in the slipperiness and the smell and the heat and the sheer wantonness of it all.

Throughout the day they held each other tightly.

Ferne lay on top of Tang on the sitting-room carpet feeding him with fruits. He sat over her, stretching her open and feeding her with a banana. Then, amid her shrieks and wriggling, he ate it out of her.

He beat her with the fly swat as they chased through the flat, gambolling on the beds, scrabbling on the floors to get away from each other's clutching.

Tang allowed her to tie him up. She bound his wrists, and hitched him to the bed head. Then she took him long and slow, savouring every second of having him inside her without him being able to retaliate.

Then he tied her hands behind her back and made her kneel with her head to the carpet and her bottom in the air. He whacked her bottom with the fly swat until it was burning red and tingling. Then he took the belt of her dressing gown to her and stroked her labia with that. They were already swollen with the excitement, and each time they felt the gentle lash of the belt they quivered with the sheer erotic pleasure of it.

When he entered her, his shaft was cool compared with the heat that he had generated. And she was moist from the stimulation and cried out as he drove himself deeply into her. He came copiously, just as Mai Lin had said he would.

They played such games all day. Rolling around like two adolescents, laughing loudly, cuddling and cajoling until they both were tired.

When it was time to take Tang home, they did not let go of each other once. In the lift they stood closely, kissing and fondling. They held hands tightly on the Tube and along the pavement as they walked to Mai Lin's house. And when she mounted the steps Ferne was crying, tears running down her cheeks, her hands shaking violently. She turned and kissed his lips, whispering, 'My God, Tang – how am I going to live without you?'

Chapter Ten

'*HOW ARE THINGS* going, Robert?'

Robert Trenchard looked grey and tired. He looked as tired as Ferne felt.

'Fine, Miss Ferne. Everything's just fine. I approved the deal we were doing with the Ministry. I hope that was all right with you.'

She waved graciously and contrived a smile. 'Of course, Bob. We'd worked out all the details, hadn't we?'

'It was just as we agreed.'

'Good. I'm sorry I couldn't be here to help. I wasn't . . .' Ferne sat back. She hated lying. But his expression told her that he didn't require an explanation from her. Normally she would never have given one, but now she felt almost compelled to. She was not a closed-up, self-important person any more.

'How about the Hagenite shares, Bob?'

He shook his head.

'It's tricky. I've lost more sleep over that than on anything I can recall recently.'

'I'm sorry, Bob. It's just that . . .'

'I know, Miss Ferne. I'll keep at it. You know I don't give up on things that easily. Now – your programme today is . . .'

The morning briefing went past Ferne without stopping. She hardly caught a glimpse of it. Pictures of Tang's boyish face kept floating before her. Recalled sensations of his body, his phallus, the way he had held her and loved her and taken her so demandingly kept encroaching on her mind. It had all been so beautiful.

Now he was gone. Ferne had never felt so alone in her life. Her body craved his as she sat there, her eyes looking at Trenchard but her mind in Mai Lin's salon.

But I told you, Cleopatra dear, that I could not spare him for more than a week.

But Mai Lin, can't you let me have him as a friend? I'll pay you well. I'll pay him a good salary too. I'll take care of him and I'll—

Mai Lin's hand had gone up. Ferne had known that was a gesture of finality. She had experienced it before. Then Mai Lin had spoken softly and with great kindness.

Tang is too valuable, Cleopatra. Do you not see? If you want him so badly after only one week, how many more women will want him too? He is priceless.

Ferne's blood ran cold as she recalled the words. She had stood, white-faced, her knuckles clenched with anger.

You bloody mercenary bitch, she'd said as her hand had struck out blindly. Without thinking she had gone to strike Mai Lin but had forgotten that her mentor was an expert in self-defence. In a second she had been on her stomach on the floor, a hard heel in the crook of her neck, her arm bent up almost to breaking point.

Mai Lin had whispered. *I do not wish to hurt you, darling. Will you get up and promise not to be naughty again?*

Ferne had never felt so small. Even under Samson's powerful hand she had not been so humbled. She had risen with tears in her eyes.

I'm sorry, Mai Lin. But I . . .

Mai Lin had hugged her.

I understand. But you must find a man of your own. Buying love is never satisfactory. It is only an interim solution to a pressing need. When you have finished here, you must solve your needs yourself. In a year, Tang will be his own man. He will be free to choose his path in life. If he continues with what I have taught him, he will become rich, and that alone will be reward enough for me. He will have the choice to work here and make his fortune, or to leave. Of course he will pay me well, but he will not be mine.

Ferne had looked at her with awe.

I found Tang living under a broken ox cart when he was ten. I have given him a life. He has love and he loves. He tells me that you have been the most wonderful woman that he has ever experienced. Does that not warm your heart?

It had, but it had driven the dagger of loneliness deeper at their parting. Only Mai Lin's reassurance that she could have Tang occasionally, on a fee-paying basis for a night, had eased the pain. But she didn't want that. She wanted him.

'And then, Miss Ferne, there is the Battered Women's Hostels committee you asked to see about donating funds. I've scheduled them at four.'

Snapped out of her reverie, Ferne looked up at Trenchard.

'Thanks, Bob. Now, I suppose I'd better get down to some dictation. Can you send Muriel in, please.'

Johnny hadn't rung all week. Jan had called her briefly, once.

Ferne toyed with a salad her secretary, Muriel, had brought down from the canteen, but it only served to remind her of the last meal Tang had made for her so lovingly.

Afterwards, they had lain naked on the sitting-room floor playing noughts and crosses. He had beaten her every time. And in his joy he had straddled her, beating his chest, his hard shaft bouncing before her eyes.

She had sat on his lap, impaled on him, listening to Beethoven as he had fondled her breasts and worked the vibrator between her legs. It had been loving. She had not needed to come but just to have him available, and for him to touch her intimately all the time.

He had made her open and uninhibited. She had not an ounce of shame or shyness left. They had practised self-defence in the nude, and she had become quite expert. At first he had always beaten her when he wanted to. She had been glad because it always ended in him entering her just to show her his prowess. But later when she had beaten him, she had straddled him and taken him into herself to turn the tables on him.

He had been more pleased at that than at anything else she had done. It had been an entirely selfless praise and she guessed that he was proud of his pupil.

Then, in a flurry of arms and legs, and pinching and tickling fingers, he had trussed her with the vacuum cleaner flex so that her arms were behind her back, her knees on her breasts, her sex open to him. Helpless as she was, he had put her on the end of her bed and had sat on the floor looking at her intimately, simply admiring her for ten minutes or more. Then he had touched her gently, outlining her labia with small, circular motions, around and around and up and down until she had squirmed.

His tongue tip had tickled her clitoris until she had demanded greater pressure, and then he had stood over her. Rapidly working himself up to orgasmic rigor, he had fountained between her legs, setting a warm line of his seed through her furrow. She could almost feel it now as she pushed her untouched salad to the side of her blotting pad.

When he had finished pumping, he had sat at the end of the bed again, sensuously massaging his fluid into her labia, over her nubbin and into the hollows of her loins. She had climaxed achingly with the sheer lasciviousness of it all, then they had lain and cuddled before showering, the time of their parting getting ever closer.

In desperation now, Ferne punched the keypad on her phone.

'Hello, Mai Lin.' She fiddled with her blotter nervously. It was the first time she had called the house since Mai Lin had given her the number some days ago. It had been a hard-won concession from the mistress of the house.

'Cleopatra? How nice of you to call.'

'Mai Lin, I need Tang. I need him desperately. Can I have him tonight? Please?'

'I'm sorry, Cleopatra, but he is not free.' The voice was hard. It was as if Mai Lin was denying her on purpose.

'But I need him.'

'You need love, Cleopatra. I saw it in your eyes. You have had sex in many ways and you have soaked it up avidly. There is little more I can teach you. But from what Tang tells me, you need someone permanent in your life, someone with common interests and goals and desires who wants you as much as you want him. No matter how long you kept Tang, he could never fulfil that need. He loves you but he does not want you as a permanent mistress.'

The words acted on Ferne like a torpedo penetrating deeply into her, exploding in a blast of broken dreams. My God, she had never thought of what Tang had wanted. She had assumed that he loved her as much as she had come to love him.

But of course – like Johnny – he had other women to practise his charm on and to make writhe in ecstasy under him. Damn. She hit the desk hard with a whitened fist.

'But what do I do, Mai Lin? I don't know what to do with myself. I'm a nervous wreck. I've got no one but you to turn to. Can I at least see Mark?'

'I'm sorry, Cleopatra, but that is not for me to say. You are Johnny's protégée. I act only under his orders in this matter.'

'But Mai Lin, I thought you were my friend. You were my lover.'

'Of course, darling, and after Johnny is satisfied with your training, we may become lovers again. I would like that. But for now I am his mistress and I take his orders.'

Ferne felt tears welling and wiped them away with the heel of her hand.

'But when will I see Johnny? He hasn't phoned me for a week.'

'I believe he's away, Cleopatra. He's overseas.'

The man next to Ferne on her settee looked dark and mysterious. At thirty something, Ramero Benud exuded a confident sexuality as his black eyes followed her movements. She fidgeted with her wineglass and found things to do: fetching nuts. Checking her hair. Making sure his glass was full when clearly it was.

Her mind hunted over all the permutations of how they were going eventually to get into bed. Or would he take her here? Perhaps he would tell her to come into the bedroom when he was ready for her. She might say, *I'll just go and slip into something more comfortable*, and wait for him, the duvet up to her chin. Would he be forceful with her? Gentle? Overbearing? His handsome Mediterranean features held an air of superiority. Did he despise the women he had sex with?

Ferne had hugged her teddy bear in bed for the last two nights. Isolated from Mai Lin and from Johnny, she desperately needed Jan to call her. But he was clearly still overseas too, his Ferrari missing from the basement garage. She had phoned his secretary to check when he would return, using a false name to avoid detection. All she had got had been a courtesy message and a *May I ask him to call you when he returns?*

In desperation she had called an 'escort' agency and this was the result.

Benud sipped his chianti and studied her languorously. He was amused by her, his eyes smiling lazily, assured of his pleasure. She didn't want to be amusing or a dead-cert lay. She wanted to be sensual. She wanted to be desirable for herself, and she recalled Mai Lin's words – *Buying love is never satisfactory. It is only an interim solution to a pressing need*. Now Ferne began seriously to doubt her actions. But her need was pressing. It was bearing on her with such force that she could hardly contain it. Her jokes to Johnny about jumping on the office boy had almost come true. Now here she was, sitting nervously with a man who was eyeing her up as if she were a strumpet.

Perhaps she was a strumpet. She was a whore except for the fact that she had payed him instead of him paying her.

He broke her thoughts by taking her glass out of her hand, setting it purposefully on the coffee table.

'Now, Cleopatra, I think we've fenced enough, don't you? What would you like me to do for you?'

My God, what would she like him to do for her? She didn't know what she wanted. Her head spun, her stomach turned over.

'I – I . . .'

He took her hand and slipped it between his legs. She trembled at the touch of his hardness.

'How do you like to be taken by a man, Cleopatra? Long and slow, or hard and brutally?'

Oh my God. How did she like to . . . ?

He slipped his zip down and slid her hand inside his trousers. It trembled more to feel the familiar hardness. She closed her eyes and breathed deeply. He was hot and he was huge.

Her hand closed on it.

He smiled.

She trembled violently now. Could she go through with this?

He moved so that she could delve deeper. A thick hand stroked her cheek, traced the outline of her lips, ran down her neck into the cleavage of her blouse.

She breathed in sharply with the touch.

His finger undid the buttons one by one. He did it slowly so that she felt each give way, her breasts becoming more visible, and more available, with each release.

The heat of his sac in her hand made her fingers curl. They had become addicted to the feel of testes retracting to her touch. It was as if she had magic in her fingers. The heel of her hand rubbed down his shaft, but there was no mobile foreskin. Her fingers told her that there was just a large and fleshy knob sitting on top of a very thick stem. Anyway, he was circumcised.

So what? It would probably feel the same inside her. If she ever got it inside her. What the hell was she doing touching a stranger and letting him fondle her? His hand was on her left breast now, pulling at the nipple, his mouth glistening as he licked his lips. Oh God, he was drooling over her.

As he rose and slipped down his trousers, the thick shaft sprang out, purple and pulsing. He was covered in hair, black and thickly matted, almost a layer of felt running from under his scrotum, around his shaft, and over a stomach now bared as he parted his shirt. She could imagine it rasping her breasts. It would be like being rubbed up by a carpet.

Her skirt was up, her knickers down in a flash as he pulled her flat on the settee, unprotesting but still uncertain. He was getting steamed up, his eyes sparking with the sight of her breasts lolling out of the open blouse, her mound naked under his gaze.

Ferne was wet with anticipation, but shaking with trepidation too. Did she really want this?

She decided not just yet as the thick stalk loomed over her and he parted her legs with his knees and bore down with his hands on her shoulders.

But now he was in her, driving deeply. She wriggled and tried to get free, but it only made him drive more.

'No. No, please. I've changed my mind.'

He laughed and pushed into her deeper.

'They often say that. You'll love it in a minute, darling. When I fill you, you'll scream for more.'

His 'darling' didn't sound like Mai Lin's darling, or Johnny's, either. It sounded chauvinistic and condescending.

'Get off, you brute. I'll have you for rape.'

He laughed again and bore into her. 'Oh no, sweetheart. Why do you think I asked you to sign the disclaimer?'

Yes, she had signed a paper which said she had hired him for sex and had paid him. But she could still throw him out.

Now they rolled from the settee. His breath was knocked out of him as they landed. It gave Ferne the chance that she needed.

Springing up, she leapt the settee and stood with it between them. He grinned and came after her, his phallus wagging menacingly. But as he caught her wrist, his glee turned to horror. She spun him in a forward roll, landing him on his back, her knee at his throat, his arm twisted painfully tightly. Tang had taught her well. And now she grabbed a fistful of his testicles and held on tightly. It gave her a surge of power as she tightened her grip and felt the man tremble.

'Now, mister, you take your money and go or I'll break your neck and screw these off. Understand?'

He nodded stiffly under her knee.

She let him up, stood back and watched as he tucked himself into his trousers, glowered at her and slammed out of the door. Ferne stood shaking. Thank God for Tang's tuition. What the heck had she been thinking of anyway? Was she in such a desperate state?

An hour later she sat hugging a cup of cocoa, her nerves more steady, trying to work out what was going on inside her.

Mai Lin had said that she needed love, and to find a man with similar interests and ambitions to her own. Someone she could share with? But what did she do in the meantime?

Johnny broke the tension with a call, the ringing phone nearly making her jump out of her skin.

'Hello, lassie. How are you doing?'

'Bloody terrible. Why?'

'Whoops. Sorry I asked. What's up, Cleo?'

'Nothing's bloody well "up", as you so aptly put it. I'm as frustrated as a bitch on heat. And you, you sod, are never around when I need you. Now – you started me off on this charade, and I want you to start taking some responsibility for what you've done. I'm sick to death of your cloak-and-dagger nonsense. Where the hell are you, for God's sake?'

Silence.

'Did you hear me, Johnny?'

'Loud and clear, Cleo. Loud and clear.'

'Well?'

'Well, it was you who wanted to stay incognito, not me.'

He was right. But her need to keep her identity a secret seemed unimportant now.

'I need you, Johnny. I'm spinning out of control.'

'Cleo, I told you that once you let the pussycat out of the cage it might turn out to be a tiger.'

'Cut the crap and tell me what you're going to do about the tiger. It was you who let it out.'

'Whoa there, lady. Who threw herself at me at Fanni's party?'

'I didn't.'

'You didn't put up much of a fight.'

'Don't say you didn't like it. Anyway, I paid you ten thousand pounds to give me some experience.'

'I said I would help you find yourself, I didn't say I would be responsible for what you found. So just settle down.'

'I can't settle down. I'm pacing the room. I suggest you come round here and finish what you started.'

'I can't.'

'Are you still abroad?'

'No, I'm in Town, but . . .'

'But nothing. Just you get round here or I'll never speak to you again.'

'No, Cleo. I can't do that.'

'Why not? I want you, Johnny. Can't you understand that?'

'I understand. But you need someone to love you, not just screw you.'

'Don't be crude.'

'Don't you be a prude. You've lapped up the sex. Now it's time to stop and take stock.'

'What does that mean?'

'It means that you've graduated in the sex department. It's time you went out and found a reliable, compatible mate.'

'Are you saying I'm not going to see you again?'

'I was ringing to say that I've arranged the last session for you.'

'That's very gallant of you.'

'Don't be sarcastic. It doesn't become you.'

'Pig.'

'Neither does that.'

'But will you be there?'

'I'll try.'

'Please, Johnny?'

'All right. Now be a good girl and relax a bit. I'm arranging a graduation party for you.'

'What kind of party? Not like the one at Fanni's.'

'No. Just a few friends at Mai Lin's.'

'I'm not sure if I want any more of that.'

'Okay. If that's how you feel. You don't have to come.'

'If I don't come, will I see you again?'

'No, Cleo.'

'That's blackmail.'

'Yes, it is. But I have something I want to tell you. Something very important.'

'Tell me now.'

'I can't. I need to see you.'

'Without my mask?'

'No, not without our masks.'

'All right. When?'

'Saturday at seven at Mai Lin's. Sleep tight, pussycat.'

'But Johnny . . . ?'

Ferne was still angry with Johnny as she walked the last few yards to Mai Lin's house. He'd baited a trap for her with a mystery sandwich. She knew that if she didn't go to Mai Lin's she would never see him again. If she did go, he said he would tell her something important. He was relying on her curiosity and her need to see him to make her go. Was he going to tell her his true identity?

Mai Lin greeted her with great affection.

Ferne hugged her but followed her along the corridors with some degree of trepidation.

The room was totally dark. Then there was a flicker in front of her. Candles? Their light gradually invaded the blackness to reveal naked people standing around a cake alive with candles.

Mark. Samson. Tang – wonderful Tang – smiling brightly at her. And there was the young couple she had spied on through the window, slender and athletic. But Johnny was not among the crowd. Her heart sank but was immediately buoyed by a cheer from the assembly. Champagne glasses were raised as Mai Lin passed her one.

'We celebrate the new Cleopatra. And your birthday, darling.' As her friends gathered around her, the question of how Mai Lin knew it was her birthday got lost among the hugs and kisses.

Mai Lin lit candles around the room.

Ferne was in tears, but they quickly turned to smiles, to merriment, and then into laughter as the champagne flowed. The cake was scrumptious and they munched grapes and ripe lychees, feeding each other as they lounged about, naked. It was as if she had come home. Gone were the frustrations, the doubts and the fears. All Ferne knew was that she was happy.

This was the best birthday party she had ever had.

Lying on the bed, Mark cuddled her, his phallus strong against her leg. They kissed and held each other tightly until the young man of the couple came and joined in. Between the two men, Ferne felt so loved. Then everyone knelt round her. Six pairs of gentle hands touched her all over, stroking and caressing, smoothing and pressing her breasts, her face, her neck, her stomach, legs and secret places.

At Mai Lin's command, Ferne was lifted and carried to an adjacent room with a pool. As the lights went out, pitch darkness enveloped them all.

Ferne swam around, her hands exploring, finding breasts afloat, curvaceous female bottoms and hard male ones. Sex-lips opened to her touch, succulent mouths osculated against hers, and a row of full-blooded erections presented themselves to her hand as if saluting her on her birthday.

They gambolled and played games, she trying to tell which man was which by the feel of his shaft. It was like playing blind man's bluff.

Samson's was easy, it was so strong and large. He held her tightly and lowered her on to it when she guessed him right. It felt so good. She felt so secure in his arms, with him embedded deeply in her.

Tang's phallus she guessed after a careful exploration, his musky-sweet scent giving him away. Immediately she found him, she tucked his shaft between her legs, pulling him to herself, running her hands over his smoothness. It was so good to have him in her arms again. Then she took him into herself, kissing him passionately, running her hands over his back and sides.

'I love you, Tang. I love you. Oh my God, I need you. Fuck me.'

There was an explosion of energy inside her as she said the words. Her whole body burst into life. In the shallows of the warm pool, he floated over her, his shaft stroking into her like waves on a shore, rushing up and receding rhythmically.

With her hair in a watery fan around her head, Ferne opened her legs and took Tang to completion. But she could not come herself. She didn't want to. She wanted to experience the others, one at a time. And she wanted to save herself for Johnny. Where was Johnny? Would he come? He had promised.

As Tang came with his usual fountain force, she floated away from him, turning to take him in her mouth to draw the last drops of seed from him. His beat in her mouth made her thrill. His moans of ecstasy made her more so. It was so much pleasure to give pleasure. If she had learned anything it was to give love in order to receive it.

After a long and sensuous time, sucking on Tang, caressing his floating pouch, he kissed her avidly as if he never wanted to let go of her. Then, finally, he led her to Mark.

Ferne knew it was Mark by the slender length of his penis. Mental pictures of how she had seen it as she had unveiled it on their first encounter came in brightly coloured waves through the darkness.

They kissed tenderly, his arms around her waist, she masturbating him seductively, the warm water multiplying the sensuality. And when she had him poker-hard and rearing, he turned her bottom to him. She felt his hardness slip though her sex-lips and ease deep into her. They floated in shallow water, her hands on the rail of the pool, Mark covering her back, biting her neck, working himself deeply inside her as the water undulated, until he flushed warmly, beating strongly in her depths with a moan of pleasure and a sigh.

As she took him in her mouth too, he tasted quite different from Tang. More earthy perhaps, with a touch of saltiness. And as he stood with legs apart, she floated on her back, pushing herself under him until she could lick his testes and tickle them naughtily.

'That's beautiful, Cleopatra. You're a wonderful lover. Do you know that?'

She smiled in the darkness. 'And you're delicious. Do you know that?'

'Thank you. And you're so beautifully tight, you make me come so easily.'

Perhaps she was 'beautifully tight'. She didn't care, and it was probably the champagne talking in both of them.

'Do you think I'm naughty?' She giggled.

'I think you're much less inhibited than when we first met.'

As she floated under Mark, licking and loving him, someone came between her legs. Hands on her bobbing breasts squeezed and kneaded gently and the unmistakable heat of a male organ at full rigidity slipped into her.

'Hello, Cleopatra, my name's Ben. I wondered when I was going to get my turn.'

Ferne's body thrilled deeply. It seemed so risqué that she had a man inside her she had never met before, and the way he kissed her deeply, his tongue lashing at hers, made her almost swoon. Then he thrust up into her and made her take a sharp breath, the warm water making the sliding of their bodies so sensuous.

She squeezed him, using all the muscle power she could muster. Still she didn't need to come, but it was marvellous just being taken with such abandon.

In the shallows, Ben became frantic. As she squeezed him he gasped and drove harder until he came, wriggling and snaking on her stomach, his hot flush warmer than the water.

He sucked on her nipples. Then he floated down and licked between her legs. Then he floated away and when he came back again, he was harder and larger and tasted different. Inside her he felt bigger, his mouth more urgent, his hands around her neck just like Johnny's hands had been as he had wrestled her and kissed her on the floor at Fanni's.

Her hand ran down his back and found a mole at the base of his spine.

'Johhnny?'

'Hello, Cleo. Are you having a nice party?'

Ferne pulled him into herself by winding her legs around his hips and crossing her ankles. There was no way she was going to let him go.

'I've missed you.'

'I've missed you too, Cleo. I'd forgotten just how wonderful you feel and taste.'

She giggled as he licked her face and she bit his neck.

In response, he drove into her deeply, his finger finding its way into her bottom.

She loved being impaled like this. It invoked such incredible pleasure-pain in her. And it took all her attention away from the annoyance she had felt at him.

Her mouth worked frantically at his now, her body fired by the mere touch of his. She had thought her attraction to Tang to be strong, but this was even stronger. He was and would always be her first lover. There was a bond between them she could not explain.

He kissed her nose, her forehead, and her chin. Then he cradled her and took her out, drying her gently and rubbing her hair.

Mai Lin had snuffed out the candles in the

bedroom. Artfully she had arranged for Johnny to come when all was cloaked in darkness.

On the bed they lay coupled again, sideways, her leg bent up around his hips. This way she was open to him, to his hand as it kneaded her bottom and slipped to her engorged love-lips. Like this, they could face each other, their breathing fanning on their mouths.

As his fingers fondled her labia, pulling her open to allow his shaft a wider access, she ran her fingers over his thigh. Now she was sure she could tell him anywhere in the dark.

'Love me, Johnny. Please, just love me for myself, not because I'm paying you.'

When Johnny turned her and spread her out, he pinned her arms above her head and took her strongly. She closed her eyes and breathed deeply with every sensuous stroke.

As his tempo increased, Ferne became enveloped in a whirling kaleidoscope of colours, of sensations, pains and pleasures. When she flooded, her body went rigid, her legs locked on to his hips, her labia squeezing on him, and she let out a scream of joy and relief.

'I love that, Johnny. Oh my God I love that so. And I love you.' She whispered it, perhaps believing that it would convince him more that way.

He stroked her hair but said nothing except a sigh.

'You don't love me, do you, Johnny?'

'I'm not Johnny, Cleo, and you're not Cleopatra. This has all been a dream – a charade. When we leave here we will go back to our other lives and this will be finished.'

'No.' She pulled him tight and gripped him so that he could not pull back from her. 'No, please don't say that.'

'I must say it, Cleo. When we started this, I thought it would be fun. I did it for a lark to teach a little iceberg a lesson. But as it's developed I've found myself more and more doubtful if it was right.'

'It was right. I was an iceberg, but I've thawed. I've never had such hot experiences in my life. I'm not the same person I was when you grabbed me out of the crowd at that dreadful party. I was a self-centred, heartless cat who couldn't love. You've set me free like you said you would.'

'I've released a tiger you can't control.'

'The tiger is tamed now. Don't you see, it was the frustration of not having you, and of not having Tang and Mark and Mai Lin. I needed them as much for the love they showed me as for the sex. But I love you too. Without you, this would never have happened to me.

'But you don't know me, Cleo.'

'I don't care. I still need you.'

'You need Johnny, sweetheart. But Johnny doesn't exist. He's just a character in a dream you've been having.'

'It's not a dream. It's real. I can feel your cock inside me still. I want to keep seeing you and having you and having you have me. Why can't we do that?'

He pulled away.

'No, Cleo. It's over, don't you realise that? I can't keep this up any more. It's driving me crazy.'

'Please don't be cross.'

He kissed her forehead. 'I'm not cross with you, Cleo. I'm cross with myself. I've betrayed us both and I hate myself for it.'

She pulled him tight again but he pulled away.

'Please, Cleo. I must go. You must find a man you can love and make a life with.'

'You're married?'

'No.'

'You're gay?'

He laughed. 'Bisexual maybe. I can love many people.'

'Then why not love me as well?'

'Because I don't want to hurt you any more than I may have done already.'

He moved out of range of her.

'You haven't hurt me, Johnny. You've given me a new life.'

Ferne grasped for him in the blackness but found nothing.

He had gone.

A cry of agony swelled in her throat and bubbled over.

'Johnny?

JOHNNY!'

Chapter Eleven

ROBERT TRENCHARD DIED at midnight on Ferne's birthday.

She sat at the hospital bedside holding his hand tightly and listening to his stertorous breathing. It was as if he were gasping for life.

His eyes opened, stared into space for a few seconds and then turned to Ferne. 'Hello, Miss Ferne. Thank you for coming. I'm sorry to be a nuisance but you're the only person I've got now.'

Tears welled in Ferne's eyes but she willed them back. This was no time to be showing her old friend her grief.

'Why didn't you tell me you had a dicky heart, Bob? I would have taken some of the load off you.'

He smiled at her lovingly. 'I wanted to see you well established, my love. You're father charged me with the task on his death bed, but it was one I took on with a happy heart.'

She closed her eyes for a second. Her father had put a great burden on many people without any thought of what it might do to them. Thank God she had started to change.

'Your father was very ambitious for you, Ferne.'

'Are you sure, Bob? Wasn't it more that he couldn't bear to see the Company broken up and sold off if I didn't run it?'

A thin smile formed on the blue-tinged lips. 'You always were a clever girl, Ferne. I'm pleased that you're changing. I was afraid not long ago that you were going to turn out to be as cold and as callous as your father.'

She squeezed his hand. 'No chance, Bob. Not with your guidance.'

Now he smiled more widely. Then the eyes went glazed and he looked into the distance. It was as if he was seeing something or someone there whom she could not see. He wracked with coughing and then wheezed, catching his breath again before he spoke.

'Tell me Ferne – is it young Van Hagen?'

'What do you mean?'

He smiled again and fixed the pale eyes on hers. He had always been able to winkle the truth out of her with that look. 'Are you not in love with Jan?'

Was she? She loved Johnny. But Johnny was gone. Mai Lin had refused to give her his name or his number. She had simply said *Go and find a man you can love, Cleopatra*.

'I was desperately in love with Jan when I was younger, Bob. You know that. I followed him about like a love-sick lamb. But when he went away and married some other girl, I was so terribly hurt, I never wanted to see him or hear about him again.

I was gutted and never thought I could forgive him. Never.'

'And now?'

'I don't know. I'm so confused. I thought I was in love with another man until tonight. Now he's deserted me just as Jan did all those years ago.'

He squeezed on her hand and concentrated hard. 'There are things you may not know, Ferne. I think I should tell you before I go. Listen to me carefully.'

She leaned close so that she could hear through his rasping.

'Your father was a jealous man. Your mother bore the brunt of that. When she turned to Jan's father for comfort, your father was outraged. He forbade her ever to speak to Henri Van Hagen again.'

'I didn't know that, Bob. But how did that affect me?'

'Your father was insanely jealous of you too. He wanted you for himself. Any young man courting you would have been turned away.'

She looked at him with disbelief. She had never realised that about her father, even though he had been so hard on her.

'And when he realised that you were seeing young Van Hagen, he threw a fit.'

'He beat me, Bob. I've still got the scars, both physical and emotional.'

Trenchard shook his head sorrowfully. 'I didn't know that. I'm so sorry.'

'But then Jan went away to Harvard, and that

was the end of us. I never heard from him once although he recently told me that he wrote nearly every day.'

The old man's eyes watered. 'He did, Ferne. Your father blocked his phone calls and had the housekeeper burn his letters. She told me so.'

Sickening, cloying darkness clamped Ferne's chest and welled up over her, blotting out the brightly lit hospital side room. She steadied herself and opened her eyes to see Robert Trenchard scanning her face anxiously.

'I'm sorry, Ferne. I thought perhaps you knew.'

She shook her head. Jan had said he'd written and she hadn't believed him. Now it was over a week since he'd contacted her. Had he gone out of her life too? She must find him and see if he still wanted her.

Robert stroked her hand with his thumb. 'I got that last of Van Hagen's shares you wanted, Miss Ferne. You've got control now.'

It was a hollow victory, coming in the wake of the news he had just cast at her. She breathed deeply and thought how little she wanted the responsibility now. The thought of vying with Jan and his Board was something she just could not contemplate.

'It was a strange thing, Ferne. The broker said Van Hagen had withdrawn his offer for the shares. He was no longer interested in buying.'

Her heart went cold. Then Jan had given up. He had stopped fighting her. Had he stopped fighting for her, too?

Ferne squeezed Robert Trenchard's hand again. 'Thanks, Bob. You've helped more that I can say.'

He smiled wanly. 'Take your chances, Ferne. I never did. I was always too busy with my career. My girl didn't wait for me. Van Hagen would be so good for you. He's the only man I know who could outsmart you. And don't be put off by that Yankee accent of his. When he dropped it once, his voice was as English as it ever was – deeper, but very English.'

'He always was good at accents, Bob. He's a natural actor.' She closed her eyes as the thought struck her.

Robert Trenchard squeezed her hand lovingly. 'If only you two could reconcile your differences, you'd make an indomitable team. From what I saw in Van Hagen's eyes when he asked me how you were, I could have sworn that he was deeply in love with you. I think he'd do anything in the world to win you. Anything.'

'Yes, Bob. I think he would – the devil. Just wait until I catch up with him.' She kissed the old man tenderly. He smiled, closed his eyes and let out a small, sighing breath as he died.

An achingly long drive from the hospital left Ferne a lot of time to fit pieces into a puzzle which had been challenging her for some time. A call to Fanni had furnished the last piece.

It was three in the morning when she hammered on Jan Van Hagen's door. There was no reply. Perhaps he was still away. She banged again, louder, again and again, while tears ran freely down her cheeks. Then, just as she was about to walk down the corridor to her own flat, Van Hagen opened his door, bleary-eyed and yawning, clad only in very briefest of briefs.

'Ferne? What the . . . ?'

She fell into his arms, and as he caught her, the dam of sorrow she had held together burst.

'Ferne?' He stroked her hair as he held her to his naked chest. 'Ferne, what's the matter?'

She took a deep breath and looked up into his eyes. 'Bob Trenchard has just died.'

They sat on his couch while she sobbed, his arms tightly around her, his tongue licking away the saltiness of her tears. He smelled so fresh and invigorating, and as her hurt and sadness ebbed away, all the little clues she had had, and had ignored, finally fell into place. But her initial anger had gone.

'I know the truth, Jan.'

'About the shares?'

'About everything.'

'I'm sorry, Ferne, but I . . .'

She put her finger to his lips. 'Shhh. Let's not talk about being sorry. I know all about it, and that's enough.'

His smile flushed away his sorrow. 'I thought you'd work it out. You're a clever girl, Ferne Daville.'

'Not so much of the girl. I was twenty-six yesterday.'

He kissed her nose. 'I know you were. Many happy returns of yesterday.'

'I had a wonderful party. Some very dear friends threw it for me.'

'I'm glad.'

As she reached up and kissed him, he took her mouth in a long and loving series of little bites.

'I love you, Jan. I suppose I always did.'

'And Johnny?'

'Johnny and I are finished. He was just a dream. He was an escape. I've been living in a fantasy world for weeks. Now I have to start living for the first time in my life and build a real relationship.' She looked around the room. Packing cases stood everywhere. The wall shelves were quite bare and cupboards stood open and empty. Suitcases by the door had luggage labels on them. Suddenly, she panicked.

'Jan? Jan, where are you going?'

He looked down on her sorrowfully. 'I'm leaving. I decided that it wasn't a very good idea to move in so close to you. I'm going to my parents' place until I can sort out somewhere else.'

Ferne sat bolt upright. 'But why? You're running out on me again. I thought that you had more guts than that.'

He nodded. 'So did I. But I found that I could not stop thinking about you just on the other side of that wall, and yet so far away.'

She stroked his face. 'I'm sorry. I've been a bitch. Please don't go, Jan. I've lost two of my dearest friends today, and I couldn't bear to lose you as well.'

He took her in his arms with relief and held her tightly.

'I love you Ferne. I knew we were destined for one another, that's why I wouldn't give up on you before. Do you blame me?'

She slipped her hand around his naked waist and held him close, snuggling into his neck.

'Bob told me before he died how you'd withdrawn from buying the last shares. Why?'

'I wanted you more than those shares, sweetheart.' He squeezed her gently. 'So, you've won. You're my boss now.'

She shook her head. 'There's not going to be a boss. A good marriage consists of give and take. Isn't that what you said?'

'Something like that. Are you proposing to me, Ferne Daville?'

'Would you have me if I did?'

The passionate five minutes of kissing spelled yes.

'I suppose you'll want your ten thousand from the wager,' he asked between bites on her neck and kisses on her lips.

'I won't keep you to that.'

'It's yours. A bargain is a bargain.' Reaching out, he took an envelope off a coffee table and put it in her hand. 'I had it ready for you if you came gloating.'

She gave him a playful push and opened the envelope, looked at the contents and smiled. 'Thanks, Jan. That's so generous of you. That's the best engagement present I could ever have had. Now – are you going to take me to bed?'

With the envelope clutched in her hand, he

lifted her, and took her to his bed. Carefully he put the envelope on the cabinet beside her. Then he removed her blouse, putting his mouth to her neck, and her breasts, taking her stiff nipples one by one.

She felt a tremor run through her stomach to her clitoris. Already it was coming awake and she only needed to have him touch it to make it fully erect. Strangely, all her hurt had gone.

She slipped her hand inside his briefs, cupped his warm sac and caressed it briefly. The stiff shaft of his penis met her finger tips. She ran them down its length, pulling his foreskin up and pushing it down again with slow and gentle strokes. Now she eased away his briefs, kissing at the head of his phallus as it emerged, licking at his testicles as she whisked the briefs away to leave him naked, smiling down at her.

She pushed back his legs and opened him up to her gaze, and kissed his balls and took them gently in her mouth. He closed his eyes in ecstasy. Now she raised herself, took the head of his shaft between her lips and suckled on it, tonguing the groove and making it pulse with every lick.

He moaned again and took a long and satisfied breath.

When she worked her way up his body, kissing his belly and his breasts, he combed her hair with his fingers. And when they had kissed long and hard, he knelt over her, pulling off her trousers to bare her completely. Now he spread her legs and pushed them back just as she had done to him. He kissed the insteps of her feet and slowly set a line of little kisses up her legs. When he reached the expanse of taut skin of her loins, she spread her legs wider, opening up her sex to him, wanting to feel his mouth on the labia, his tongue deep inside her.

As he breathed deeply of her scent and put his tongue tip out, she wriggled down to touch it, working her hips so that it licked across her clitoris and into her labial groove.

Now he sank between her legs and stayed there, kissing and caressing her, and taking little sucking lip-bites at her clitoris.

She kneaded his hair with one hand and worked her breast with the other, pulling up her nipple, and pinching it between her thumb and finger. And as he bit playfully at the tensioned skin between her engorged labia and her loins, she giggled, the tension of the past few days completely gone.

Deep inside her, his tongue felt more marvellous in a way than any shaft could do. It wiggled and it tickled, making her heave her pelvis upwards and splay her legs right out.

As the mouth came sucking and biting upwards, she pulled his ears to make the progress faster, to feel the heat of his chest against hers again, and to feel the stiffness of his shaft.

Now he ploughed it through her sexual groove, running it up and over her clitoris, stroking the standing bud with the tip before retreating again. Again and again he rubbed her while she moaned and thrust up her breasts.

When finally he changed angle and let the tip of his phallus nose about the entrance of her sex, she sank down on it. She took him in, closing on him with her newly trained muscles until he sighed with the delight of it.

Then, when he took her arms above her head and pinned her down with his mouth on hers, she thrust her pelvis upwards in a series of ripples, closing on him each time, squeezing on his shaft.

'My God, Ferne Daville, you've got some explaining to do.'

She laughed.

'Am I not the inexperienced little thing you expected?'

He bit her neck. 'You're marvellous. Now stop wriggling so provocatively on my cock or I'll come before I've had my fill of you.'

'Until I've had my fill of you, don't you mean? Fill me, Jan. Let me feel all of you.'

He thrust deeply, the root of his shaft pressing hard against her clitoris, giving it the erotic punishment it seemed to need.

She whispered in his ear.

'Fuck me, Van Hagen, you animal. I need your heat.' She contracted her muscles on him.

'My God, Ferne you're a firecracker. Where did you learn to squeeze like that?'

'You'd be surprised.' She laughed and squeezed again.

He thrust in hard. 'You're wonderfully tight.'

'It's funny you should say so,' she giggled. 'A friend recently told me exactly the same.'

'But I always thought you were such a well-brought-up girl.'

'Well, it seems that you were wrong, Van Hagen. I haven't been marking time since you went away, you know.'

He forced her legs back and stretched her sex widely, and drove down into her with long, slow strokes.

She squeezed on every in-stroke and opened herself as he pulled away.

'Squeeze me again,' he whispered. 'Whoever taught you to use your charms like that knew what he was doing.'

'He was a beast,' she sighed, and clawed Van Hagen's back. 'He was a low-down, deceitful pig.'

In retaliation, he increased the tempo of his strokes as she gripped his shaft with her vaginal muscles, and his buttocks with her clawing fingers, pulling him into herself.

The bed began to shake as their bodies repeatedly meshed and parted. Their panting rose to a crescendo of moans and cries of 'Ohh' and 'Ahhh'.

She bit and clawed, goading him to such a frenzy she was set alight by it. The power that she had found to inspire her men had proved addictive and now she used it to the full.

He lifted her under the buttocks with his hands, turned her sex-mouth upwards, plunging down into her with such ardour she rolled her head and bucked upwards. The familiar finger drove into her behind, intensifying the waves of heat spreading up from her burning clitoris. And when they both climaxed in a welter of their sweat, his semen, her tears and sexual nectar, the scents of musk mixed with aftershave filled their nostrils and their lungs.

With her man on top of her, beating deeply between her closed legs now, kissing at her neck, Ferne reached out and took the envelope from the bedside table. She screwed up the cheque for ten thousand pounds which she had written for her tuition at Mai Lin's all those weeks before. Then she ran her hand down Jan's long, lithe back. Here she found the mole right at the bottom of his spine, and caressed it lovingly before she fell asleep.

Jan or Johnny – what did a name matter now?

LITTLE, BROWN & CO. ORDER FORM

All X Libris titles are £4.99

Little, Brown and Company, PO Box 50,
Harlow, Essex CM17 ODZ
Tel: 01279 438150   Fax: 01279 439376

Payments can be made as follows: cheque, postal order (payable to Little, Brown and Company) or by credit cards, Visa/Access. Do not send cash or currency. UK customers and B.F.P.O. please allow £1.00 for postage and packing for the first book, plus 50p for the second book, plus 30p for each additional book up to a maximum charge of £3.00 (7 books plus). Overseas customers including Ireland, please allow £2.00 for the first book plus £1.00 for the second book, plus 50p for each additional book.

NAME (Block Letters) ....

....

ADDRESS ....

....

....

☐ I enclose a cheque/postal order made payable to Little, Brown and Company for £_____

☐ I wish to pay by Access/Visa/AMEX* Card
(* delete as appropriate)

Number ☐☐☐☐☐☐☐☐☐☐☐☐☐☐☐

Card Expiry Date_____ Signature_____